THE GREEK'S
SECRET HEIR

THE GREEK'S
SECRET HEIR

REBECCA WINTERS

MILLS & BOON

First published in Great Britain 2020
by Mills & Boon, an imprint of HarperCollins*Publishers*
1 London Bridge Street, London, SE1 9GF

www.harpercollins.co.uk

HarperCollins*Publishers*
1st Floor, Watermarque Building,
Ringsend Road, Dublin 4, Ireland

Large Print edition 2021

© 2021 Rebecca Winters

ISBN: 978-0-263-29002-8

MIX
Paper from
responsible sources
FSC www.fsc.org **FSC™ C007454**

To my darling children.
They're so supportive,
I'm the luckiest mum in the world!

PROLOGUE

"Monika? I'm so hot I'm going for a quick swim before I'm burned to a crisp."

Her sandy-haired friend didn't open her eyes. "I'll join you in a few minutes."

Alexa Remis, almost eighteen, got up from one of the rental loungers set out along the semicrowded Perea Beach outside Salonica, otherwise called Thessaloniki, Greece. The August temperature had climbed to the high eighties, perfect for her three-week vacation before school started again on Cyprus, nearly a thousand miles away. This was only her second day of freedom from books and tests, but it would go too fast and she wanted to make the most of it.

After wading into a surreal world of turquoise water, she kept going until she could immerse herself in the deepening cobalt blue beyond. Talk about paradise! On impulse she did a series of somersaults and ended up colliding with a hard, male body who gripped her arms to steady her.

"I'm sorry!" she cried after lifting her head. Once he let go, Alexa had to tread water to stay afloat.

"It was my fault, *despinis*." The sincere apology, spoken in Greek, came from the gorgeous guy staring straight into her eyes. In the afternoon sun she couldn't tell if his eyes were black or brown between those black lashes. "I'm Nico Angelis."

"I'm... Mara Titos." She'd almost made her first mistake by telling him her real name. Her grandfather was the Greek ambassador in Nicosia in Cyprus. For security reasons he and her grandmother had made her promise never to reveal who she really was to anyone while on vacation. With so much political unrest there, they didn't want Alexa to be a target for enemies.

Meeting this Adonis out swimming had

thrown her off-balance. "Where did you come from, Nico?"

He pointed to a sleek white cruiser in the distance, revealing his well-defined chest. "My friends and I have been racing each other."

"And I ruined it for you by being in your way."

His gaze wandered over her, making her feel a voluptuous warmth that was completely different from the effect of the sun. "I didn't watch where I was going, but believe me, I'm not complaining about running into a beautiful mermaid. I didn't know they came with long chestnut hair and sea-green eyes." She smiled as he asked, "Do you live here?"

"No." *Remember what you're supposed to tell people, Alexa.* "I live in France with my mom, but am on vacation until school starts."

"You're a long way from home. I've just turned nineteen and must join the Greek navy in three weeks to do my military service."

They swam around each other. "Are you looking forward to it?"

"Not particularly. I'd much rather stay right here."

The comment sounded so personal her heart picked up speed. "How long will you have to be gone?"

"Two years." He studied her features, lingering on her lips. "At the moment a year sounds like a lifetime."

"One more year in a strict French schoolroom before college sounds like a lifetime to me too." After he chuckled, she heard voices in the distance coming from the cruiser. "I think your friends are calling to you." But Alexa didn't want their conversation to end.

"That's okay. They can wait. I have more pressing matters here." His compelling mouth broke out into a smile, turning her body to liquid. "What about you?"

Remember for security reasons that Monika has a different name too. "My cousin Leia is sunbathing. I'm staying with her and the Vasilakis family during my vacation."

"How long are you here for?"

"Three weeks."

"That's perfect. It gives us time to make some plans."

He had a masterful way about him that made her breathless. There was no guy in Europe or anywhere else who acted or looked like Nico. The dark hair plastered to his head reminded her of a copy of a statue of a young Emperor Augustus in the Archaeological Museum of Salonica she'd seen yesterday.

Monika's parents, the Gatakis, who'd only recently begun working at the embassy with Alexa's grandfather, kept a house here. They'd insisted the girls have one day of intellectual pursuits before hitting the beach for the rest of their holiday.

As far as Alexa was concerned, Nico, with his chiseled features and firm jaw, could have been a model and was so handsome, she couldn't take her eyes off him.

"What did you have in mind?" She knew she was being picked up. Other guys had tried. Before now she'd never been tempted to break her grandparents' rules, but this guy was different. She decided to go with it and see what happened.

"Tell your cousin you're swimming to the cruiser with me. I know a place along the coast where we can buy food and eat on deck while we get to know each other better. I'll bring you back before it gets too late. Wherever I'm stationed in the military, I'd like a happy memory to take with me."

That worked both ways. "What about your friends?"

"I'll drop them at the pier."

So it was Nico's boat. Alexa made a snap decision. "I'll swim to shore and let her know."

His smile faded. "If you don't come back, I'll know this meeting wasn't meant to be after all and you really are a mermaid who'll disappear on me."

Alexa took off for the beach, haunted by what he'd just said. She reached the lounger dripping wet and told Monika what had happened. "He's going to take me for a boat ride."

Her friend jumped to her feet. "Are you

crazy? Don't you know who that is?" She sounded almost angry.

"Should I?"

"Nico Angelis is the only son of the billionaire Estefen Angelis, the famous Angelis Shipping Lines owner in Salonica. I've told you about him before."

Alexa didn't remember.

"Over the last year he's been in the news—he gets around." At least Monika knew of him. Alexa's grandparents couldn't object to that. "There've been times when he's played volleyball here on the beach with some of his highbrow friends, picking up girls. He's the last guy on earth you should ever get mixed up with."

Whoa. How could Alexa have known something like that while she'd been living in Cyprus for so many years with her grandparents? "He's still out there waiting for me."

Monika laughed. "You really think so with a line like the one he just fed you? A mermaid? How naive can you get."

Alexa felt foolish. "Maybe I am. But all the

same, I'm swimming back out." She hurried into the water once more, wondering, fearing that he'd disappeared. Somehow the idea of never seeing him again disturbed her.

"Mara?"

He was still there. Alexa had almost forgotten that was the name she'd given him. She had her answer and knew she was going to spend the next few hours with him no matter what Monika said.

"Nico!"

CHAPTER ONE

Nineteen years later

ON A WARM Saturday evening in June, thirty-eight-year-old Nico Angelis drove up to the front of the Papadakis mansion in Salonica. Nico was still trying to get over the pain of losing Tio Papadakis six months ago.

They'd met in the military and became best friends. Later, they'd each served as the other's best man at their weddings. But a dinner out last December had ended in tragedy for his friend.

Tio had been driving the car that had killed him and had put his wife Irena in a wheelchair with a bruised spine. It had taken her a month to be able to walk again without help and she still used her wheelchair sometimes. Until then she'd had a health caregiver who looked after her and provided the therapy she needed.

Since the accident Nico had tried to look in on Irena and her two sons once a week. He'd lost his wife years earlier and knew the pain Irena had to be in. Nico suffered survivor's guilt over the part he'd played in his own wife's death that couldn't be erased. He didn't think it would ever go away. To be able to help Irena by talking to her about Tio made him feel like he was doing something worthwhile.

Eleven years earlier his wife Raisa and their unborn child had been killed in a plane crash. Like Tio, Nico had been at the controls when the accident occurred. For an inexplicable reason, Nico and his copilot had escaped death.

Since then, Nico had plunged into his work to deal with his pain and put away thoughts that he didn't have a child to cherish. He'd wanted their baby more than anything in this world and had been so excited for its impending birth. A son or daughter to love would have meant everything to him, but it hadn't happened.

At least Irena had her boys. Nico envied Irena that blessing and had learned to love her sons like his own. Raisa's death was something no one could fix, but he could give Irena and her boys his love and support.

Two months ago Nico's father had stepped down as head of the Angelis Shipping Lines, owing to heart trouble. Nico, one of three vice presidents at the time, had been voted in as CEO of the corporation.

Their headquarters maintained the largest cargo shipping company in the Balkan hinterland and Southeastern Europe. The Angelis conglomerate also owned several manufacturing companies and the *Halkidiki News*, a newspaper servicing Northern Greece.

It had been managed by his uncle—the brother-in-law of Nico's mother—for over a decade. But he'd caused a scandal in the family and their father had promoted Nico's thirty-six-year-old sister Giannina to executive status at the newspaper to keep him under control.

Their uncle, who'd been born a Hellenian before becoming a Greek citizen, resented a woman having that kind of power and hadn't been making it easy for her. Nico was proud of how Giannina handled their uncle as she worked her way up in administration at the newspaper.

It pleased him that their father saw her potential to be a tour de force. Now, with the responsibility of the Angelis Shipping Lines falling on his shoulders, Nico had little time for anything else besides looking after his parents and of course Irena and her boys.

These days Nico commuted to headquarters in Salonica by helicopter from his villa in Sarti eighty-seven miles away. Tonight he was running late. The housekeeper Melia let him in and told him he'd find Irena and Kristos in the salon. Apparently her younger son Yanni was over at a friend's house.

"Nico, at last!" Irena cried and held out her arms to him. He hugged her. She'd been a redheaded beauty who'd claimed Tio's heart in his teens.

Kristos got up from the couch to give him a hug. "I was afraid you might not come, Uncle Nico." Her boys had called him that for years. They'd never know how much they meant to him.

"Sorry I'm late. Already I'm learning why I rarely saw my father growing up."

"He's paid a price for it," Irena interjected. "Don't let hard work cut your life short, Nico." She stopped there, unlike Giannina who would have said she feared he didn't have any other life now. His sister worried that he hadn't found another woman and she wouldn't let it go. Nico had been involved with several women from time to time, but he'd had it with love and commitment.

"I'm not planning on it," he muttered, looking at Irena with concern. "Have you been brooding again?"

"Yes. I miss Tio more than usual tonight."

Nico could relate. "Why is that?"

"Because of me," Kristos broke in. The

handsome nineteen-year-old had grown tall like his father. Nico would have given anything for a son like him, but fate had stepped in once again the way it had done when he himself was nineteen, robbing him of any happiness for a long, long time.

"Isn't college going well for you?"

"That's not it. Mama's upset because I've met a girl and want to get engaged now. We're thinking a wedding at the end of August. By then the apartment we've settled on near the university will be free."

She shook her head. "It's way too soon for you to be so involved. Your life is only beginning, darling. I'm sure her mother would say the same thing. You need to wait several years at least. Your father would be in total agreement with me."

"That's not true, Mama. I've done my military service and have an important job in the family business. I can support us, and both our college classes are going along fine. It's not too soon. We're in love and don't want to wait."

Irena's eyes met Nico's, pleading with him to do something about this. He knew Tio's stubborn father was behind Irena's hesitation. The older man hadn't approved of Tio's marriage and was now interfering in his grandson's love life.

"What's her name, Kristos?"

"Dimitra Remis."

"Tell me about her."

His warm gray eyes lit up. "She's eighteen, smart and gorgeous."

Nico grinned. "Of course she is."

"She's barely eighteen," a troubled Irena informed him.

"Dimitra goes to the University of Salonica too, Uncle Nico. I can't begin to describe how wonderful she is."

Kristos was definitely smitten. "Tell me about her mother and father."

"Her parents are Greek. They fell in love. However, through unavoidable circumstances, they lost touch with each other and he disappeared from her mother's life before she ever knew she was pregnant."

"That's very sad." Nico thought about the unborn child he'd lost when Raisa had died. "It's tragic the man never knew he had a daughter."

"Dimitra always wanted to know him. That ache will never go away for her."

"Of course not," Nico murmured. Certain aches always remained, as Nico knew so well. His yearning to have a family of his own would always be there, but it hadn't been meant to be.

"I'm thankful I had nineteen years with Papa," Kristos broke in on Nico's thoughts. "But Dimitra has still had a wonderful life. Until last August she and her mother lived with her great-grandparents in Canada. He was the Greek ambassador in Ottawa before his retirement. Since coming back to Greece, they have a home here and her mother teaches on the faculty at the University of Salonica in the language department."

"That sounds impressive."

"You and Mama will love Dimitra. I've bought her an engagement ring she doesn't know about yet. Naturally I want to announce our engagement right away, but Mama wants us to wait."

Irena moved the wheelchair closer. "That's right, darling. You need time to do a little more living before making a decision that will change your life."

Kristos looked to Nico for the answer he wanted. "What do *you* say?"

It was like déjà vu for Nico who understood what it was like to be painfully, excruciatingly in love at that age and want to get married. But no commitment like that should be pursued at their tender age, as he had learned the hard way.

After Mara Tito had sent back all the letters Nico had written to her nineteen years ago, *unopened*, he'd gotten the message and had learned a bitter truth. The true love he'd thought they'd shared after three weeks of nonstop enchantment had only been on his part. It hadn't lasted for her. The longing to marry her and have children with her had been *his* dream, not hers.

The second he'd left to do his military service, she'd never thought about him again. He'd been a fool to think otherwise. When he and Tio had returned home a year later, she was nowhere to be found and untraceable. The phone number at the Vasilakis residence had been disconnected.

All the considerable resources at his disposal as an Angelis to do searches both here and in France had turned up literally nothing. After three difficult years of trying to forget her, he'd met Raisa Nephus and in time had married her.

When Nico thought of how happy Kristos was right now, it worried him that this girl he loved might not prove to love him with the same depth of passion. A real broken heart took years to get over, if ever...

"Uncle Nico?" Kristos prodded him.

Nico realized Irena's son was waiting to hear his view on the situation. While his friend lay dying in the hospital he'd promised Tio to look after Kristos and Yanni. Nico's first instinct was to tell Kristos he couldn't give him his blessing. To get engaged this soon could ruin the rest of his life. No one knew that better than Nico.

In time he'd learned to love Raisa enough to marry her, but it hadn't been like his feelings for Mara. Raisa had deserved more, and after she'd died in the plane he'd been flying, his guilt had intensified because he hadn't been able to save her or their baby she was carrying…

But his past life had nothing to do with Kristos. Nico and Irena needed to make a concession to her son so he wouldn't feel that the entire world had conspired against him.

"Tell you what, Kristos. Your birthday is coming up soon. Invite her over for an informal meal. I'll drop by at some point after work and you can introduce me. What do you think, Irena?" He darted her a speaking glance.

"We could do that," she said in an unenthusiastic voice, obviously deciding to go along with Nico's idea.

"Thank you, Mama! I'll call her and we'll

pick a date that's good for everyone. I prom-ise you two will love her." Kristos kissed his mother and hugged Nico before leaving the room.

Nico got to his feet. "I'm afraid I've let you down, Irena."

"No. You haven't. It was the perfect thing to say, otherwise he would have declared he and Dimitra were going to run away and get mar-ried. You've at least bought us a little more time to convince him to think about it."

"We can hope."

Deep down Nico didn't believe Kristos could be made to see reason, not if he loved this Dimitra the way Nico had loved Mara.

In time Raisa had taught him that there were different kinds of love. Though he'd never felt the fire for her he'd felt for Mara, he'd married Raisa. The excitement of a baby coming had brought him a whole new world to look forward to. Until her death they'd been thrilled at the thought of a son or daugh-ter to complete their lives.

As for Kristos, hopefully Nico could rea-

son with him to the point he wouldn't jump
into anything too fast, but he wasn't holding
his breath.

Alexa had already gotten under the covers when her brunette daughter tiptoed into
her bedroom, letting light in from the hall.
"Mama? Are you asleep?"

She chuckled. "I was getting there."

"Can we talk for a second?"

"Sure. Come sit on the bed. What's so important it can't wait until tomorrow?"

"Kristos has a birthday coming up. His
mother has invited us to dinner so we can all
meet." That *was* news. "I've never met her or
his younger brother. It's on Saturday, a week
from today. You can come, right?" Her light
green eyes implored Alexa to agree.

To meet the mother meant things were getting more serious between her daughter and
the young man Alexa had met at the university a few months ago. She'd been introduced
to him when Dimitra had brought him to her
faculty office. They'd talked for a few min-

utes and she'd learned, among other things, that his father had died in a car accident in December.

Alexa had to admit he was good-looking with a definite charm and intelligence. But after falling in love with Nico Angelis at seventeen, their brief time together in Salonica had ended in total disaster. When he'd left for the military three weeks later, he'd never gotten in touch with her again.

Four years passed before Alexa learned the true reason why he'd disappeared from her life. Because of those four years of suffering, Alexa didn't want her daughter to be thinking marriage with Kristos. Not yet. They were both very young. If anything went wrong and Kristos ended up hurting her, she didn't want Dimitra to go through that same kind of grief as Alexa at such a tender age.

"I'll have to check my schedule at the university in case there's a dinner conflict."

"Surely you can get out of it. This dinner is important to me."

She sighed. "When you're young, everything's important."

"I love Kristos."

"You'll probably love several men before you find the right one for you."

"Even if it didn't last, you fell in love with Papa when you were my age and had me."

Heaven help me. "You're right."

"Do you ever wonder where he is now or what he's doing?"

"I did in the beginning, but it's been years, honey." In truth Alexa knew exactly where Nico was and what his life was like married to an Athenian beauty. He was an Angelis and rising to the top. She'd done everything possible not to think about him over the years.

"I never stop wondering about him, Mama. What would it have been like if you'd been able to marry him. You can't deny you wanted to marry him. You told me *he* was the one for you no matter what. Right?"

Alexa moaned inwardly. "That's true, but it's also true that I was too young. Honey, you've got years to be thinking of getting married."

"I'm eighteen."

"Barely."

"I don't want to wait!" She was Alexa's daughter all right, at least the way Alexa used to be. "Please do this for me."

She patted her arm. "I'll think about it. Now go to bed. Morning will be here before we know it."

Her daughter didn't say anything else and slipped away, hurt by her mother's unenthusiastic response.

Alexa turned over and buried her wet face in the pillow. Tonight's conversation with Dimitra had brought back the past with swift, sharp pain. Only two weeks after Nico had left for military service, Alexa's grandfather Gavril had been made the Greek ambassador in Ottawa, Canada. It wasn't until they moved there from Nicosia on Cyprus that Alexa discovered she was pregnant.

As Alexa had found out, *once you started a partial truth, it lived with you forever.*

She'd wanted her daughter to grow up having a respectable background. But she was also desperate to cover her shame and embarrassment over her failed relationship at seventeen years of age with a playboy who'd never loved her. With a baby coming, the only thing she could say to people was that something unavoidable had happened that had kept her and Dimitra's father apart. They'd lost total touch with each other.

It was the same explanation she'd given her daughter when she was old enough to understand.

Alexa prayed it would stop Dimitra from asking too many questions about her father. She also hoped to avoid scandal involving Nico's prominent family, or scandal for her grandfather who held an important position in the government.

It wasn't until four years later that Monika Gataki, Alexa's teenage friend whom she hadn't heard from in several years, phoned Alexa out of the blue. She made an admission that changed Alexa's world forever. Monika admitted that she'd been so jealous of Alexa's relationship with Nico, she'd sent all his letters back unopened.

He'd honestly sent her the letters he'd promised?

The phone call sent her into shock. Alexa couldn't believe Monika had done something so horrible, so *immoral*. After four years of guilt, a repentant Monika—who didn't expect to be forgiven—couldn't stay quiet any longer.

The devastating revelation meant Alexa and Dimitra could have had a wonderful life with Nico once he'd returned from the military. After getting off the phone, she told her grandparents everything and prayed that it wasn't too late to tell Nico the truth.

But when her grandfather made inquiries through his private sources to locate Nico, he learned that Nico had recently married a woman from an illustrious family in Athens and was now an executive at Angelis Shipping Lines.

The news that her beloved Nico had recently married changed everything. It made her wonder how long it had taken him to get over her and find another woman to love.

Alexa couldn't bring herself to tell him about their daughter. Obviously he'd moved on and had found love, something Alexa never expected to find again. It hurt to know that he'd met another woman he cared about enough to marry, but Alexa didn't want to ruin his chance for happiness. To take vows meant he had embraced a new life. Did she dare disturb the life he was living now?

Could his new marriage survive the fact that he had a daughter? How would he and his wife deal with it? Alexa couldn't do that to him or to the woman he'd married. As for Dimitra, she'd been a happy, contented child since birth, protected by love and from any hint of scandal or gossip.

Even if Nico were to be told and wanted to see Dimitra, how would her daughter react? Only being four years old, would she be frightened and upset? Or would she love Nico immediately and want to be around the daddy she'd always asked about no matter what?

How would her precious daughter handle visitation when they all lived thousands of miles apart? Her little girl's life would never be the same. Alexa's instinct was to protect Dimitra to the death. In the end she decided never to tell father or daughter the truth.

But she did give Dimitra the one little two-by-two photo Alexa had taken of a handsome Nico at nineteen so she'd have something to treasure. She'd also told her he'd gone by the nickname Dino and she'd met him in Greece on vacation before leaving for Canada with her grandparents.

Alexa claimed she'd found it on a shelf in the closet among some things she'd stored. Dimitra kept it like a sacred treasure, making Alexa realize how her daughter hungered for the daddy she'd never known. Dimitra had noticed he had dark hair like her own and that made her happy.

Alexa's grandparents believed she should seek out Nico and tell him everything. They said he had a right to know he was a father, but they also said it was her decision to make. They hoped she could live with her silence. She'd assured them she could now that she knew Nico was happily married. The knowledge had helped her put her pain and feelings on hold. Her grandparents accepted her decision.

For many years she'd been forced to deal with her guilt and fought not to let it consume her. But recently everything had changed. For one thing, Alexa's grandmother had died and her grandfather had moved them back to Salonica after retirement.

Once they were settled in the home he'd bought here, Alexa had been watching the news with him. Suddenly a breathtaking picture of a dark-haired Nico Angelis flashed on the screen. He'd just been named CEO of Angelis Shipping Lines and stood with a group of officials as he christened their latest tanker. After nineteen years, the first sight of a grown-up Nico brought Alexa close to a faint.

CHAPTER TWO

NOW THAT THE FAMILY was back in Greece, it was inevitable Alexa would see an important national figure like Nico Angelis on TV. Sure enough the other night the news had shown him among a group of foreign dignitaries discussing a new water route to the east on the Aegean.

He stood a little taller than the other men. With his broad shoulders, there was no man on earth to match him. The woman he'd married had to have thought the same thing. By now he probably had several children. They'd be Dimitra's half brothers or sisters…

He'd been dashing at nineteen. At thirty-eight years of age, he'd become the quintessential Greek male. Dimitra would be astounded to learn her birth father was someone so famous and outstanding. *And impossibly appealing.*

But if at this late stage Alexa decided to divulge the truth to him and Dimitra, it could bring chaos. What if he couldn't accept his daughter in the fullest sense? Alexa would never be forgiven by either of them no matter how much she'd believed she'd done the right thing at the time. Her relationship with her daughter could be permanently jeopardized. Alexa couldn't afford to risk that.

Dimitra was her life. Because she loved her so much, she decided to relent and agree to meet Kristos's mother to avoid hurting Dimitra. They'd never had a truly serious disagreement in their lives. Considering that her daughter was head over heels in love, Alexa needed to decide which battle to fight. This wasn't one of them. Dimitra, who'd only dated a little before meeting Kristos, was only asking her to meet his mother.

She slid out of bed and padded down the hall to her daughter's bedroom. Dimitra was just coming out of the bathroom. It looked like she'd been crying.

"Mama?"

"I couldn't let you go to bed until I told you I'd be happy to have dinner with Kristos and his mother."

Following a cry of joy, Dimitra hugged her so hard she almost knocked her over.

The night of the dinner, Alexa walked into her grandfather's den wearing a white silk dress with a small blue print. He could still get around, but his arthritis was worse and at night he'd get so tired, he used a wheelchair. "I promise we won't stay out late."

"Take as long as you want."

Her daughter hugged him. "Good night, Papoú. Please don't wear yourself out." *Papoú* was the Greek word for grandfather, but it worked for her great-grandfather too.

"Don't you worry about me. Good night, sweetheart. Have a wonderful time."

Before leaving the house, Alexa gave her

grandfather a kiss, then thanked his caregiver Phyllis who lived with them.

The minute the two of them stepped outside into the soft June night air Alexa was overwhelmed by the summery fragrance unique to Salonica and it swept her back to other glorious nights here nineteen years ago.

After getting off work, Nico would come to the Gataki house to collect her and then she and Nico would go to the beach and end up in each other's arms.

Not for the first time did Alexa's daughter remind her of herself, getting ready to meet Nico for another rapture-filled night of being together. Dimitra's high spirits over the dinner ahead had brought a flush to her cheeks. But this private get-together had put Alexa on edge.

The conversation with Kristos's mother would inevitably bring up the subject of Dimitra's father. What kind of work had he been doing before they lost touch? How had they met? Alexa was ready with answers, but each time she had to explain to anyone now that they were back in Greece, it burned like a branding iron. After all these years, Alexa was back and geographically close to Nico. *Too* close.

Once in the car, she followed her daughter's directions to the Papadakis villa in the upper city. Dimitra had already told her about Kristos's mother who was still recovering after the accident that had killed her husband.

Kristos was the elder son of Tio Papadakis, who'd been one of the vice presidents of Papadakis Shipping Lines before his death six months earlier. In addition to his studies Kristos worked part-time in the family business under his CEO grandfather and hoped to rise in the business.

Alexa found it an amazing coincidence that Kristos, like Nico, had been born into a renowned Greek shipping family here in Salonica. No doubt his assured future and that of his younger brother boded well for a wonderful life.

She knew her daughter's one great wish was that both women would give their blessing for her and Kristos to be married soon. They were of legal age, but Dimitra wanted her mother to be happy about it. Of course she did.

"There it is!" her cry broke into Alexa's thoughts. "The gray-and-white mansion ahead with the statuary. Isn't it beautiful?"

"It certainly is."

"Kristos said to pull into the circular drive and park in front."

No sooner had Alexa pulled the car to a stop than a dark blond Kristos hurried out the front door and down the steps to greet them. He wore a light blue blazer over a button-down shirt and trousers. Dimitra had dressed in a yellow sundress. As Alexa had thought before when he'd come to her office at the university with her daughter, they made a good-looking couple.

He came around with Dimitra and helped Alexa out of the car. "Mama is looking forward to meeting you, Kyría Remis. We're eating outside."

She followed the two of them through the

elegant mansion and out the doors to the back patio surrounded by a flowering garden. The lovely redheaded woman in a deep blue silk dress got up from her wheelchair to greet them. "I'm delighted the two of you have come, Kyría Remis."

"We're pleased to be here and meet you, Kyría Papadakis. Thank you for inviting us."

"Call me Irena. Let's talk at the table while my housekeeper Melia serves us, shall we? My son has been impatient for this night to come."

Irena had to be close to Alexa's age with a charm her son had inherited. "My daughter has been no different."

Like coconspirators, the two women smiled at each other in understanding before Kristos assisted his mother to the candlelit round table. She walked carefully while Alexa and Dimitra found places and the four of them sat. A fifth place had been set, no doubt for her younger son.

Soon their dinner arrived and they began to

eat. "Kristos told me he met you at the university. What do you teach, Kyría Remis?"

"English to business students, and please call me Alexa."

Irena nodded with a smile. "How long did you live in Canada?"

"The whole of Dimitra's life. Once she went to first grade, I started a program to become a teacher while I attended the University of Ottawa. After my postgraduate studies, I started teaching Greek there."

"I'm very impressed."

"Don't be, but thank you, Irena." She drank some of her coffee. "When my grandmother passed away last year, my retired grandfather wanted to move back here. We came last August. Because of my experience living in an English-speaking country for so long, I joined the faculty here to teach English in a bilingual program."

"We're glad you did," Kristos interjected. "Otherwise we wouldn't have met." He couldn't take his eyes off Dimitra. Alexa had to acknowledge that like these two, she and

Nico had been just as love struck and oblivious to everything except one another.

"What are you studying at the university, Dimitra?"

"She's terrific at math, Mama."

"My least favorite subject," Irena murmured.

Alexa nodded. "And mine."

Dimitra flashed Kristos's mother a smile. "Mama says I get it from my father."

"Lucky you."

Tell the truth when you can, Alexa.

"When I met Dimitra's father, he had plans to take engineering classes in college. We were both students and met on vacation," she said without naming a location, "but were unavoidably separated. In time we lost touch."

She eyed Irena, needing to change the subject. "I'm so sorry about your husband. How wonderful that you have two devoted sons."

Irena nodded. "I'd say both you and I are lucky in the children department."

"You're right about that."

Kristos looked at his mother. "I wish Papa

were here to meet Dimitra. Why do you think Nico is so late?"

Nico? Alexa thought his brother's name was Yanni.

"Business, of course. Since becoming CEO, his life isn't his own anymore."

"But he said he'd come."

"He knows it's your birthday. I'm sure he'll phone if he can't make it. Forgive us, Alexa. We're talking about my husband's best friend, Nico Angelis."

"I call him Uncle Nico," Kristos volunteered.

"He's done everything for us since Tio passed away and said he'd drop by."

Irena kept on talking, but Alexa had gone into shock.

Nico Angelis had been the best friend of Irena's husband?

He was coming here to this house *tonight*? Would his wife be with him? No. It wasn't possible. Her body went hot, then cold. She felt sick.

"Excuse me, Irena. Would you mind if I

used your powder room for a moment? I'll be right back."

"Please. It's inside the doors on your left."

"Are you all right, Mama?"

"Yes, honey." Alexa got up from the table, praying her legs would support her before she fell into a dead faint in front of them.

Ready or not, your moment of truth has come, Alexa Remis. Pray the world doesn't come down on your head to bury you.

Nico got out of his car and only had to wait a moment before Melia answered the door. As he thanked her, Kristos came up behind her. "I was afraid you wouldn't be able to make it."

They hugged before he handed him a gift. "Happy Birthday. I would have been here earlier, but had to put out a fire at work first. You can open that later."

"Thanks. We're eating outside."

"Lead the way."

When they reached the patio, Nico walked around to kiss Irena's cheek, then glanced at the lovely young woman in the yellow dress seated at the table. Wavy brunette hair fell to her neck. With her coloring, she reminded him in a curious way of his sister Giannina. She was well-known for her beauty and could have been married long before now but for an unhappy love affair that had put her off men. He had to believe that would change in time.

"Uncle Nico? I'd like you to meet my girl-friend, Dimitra Remis."

He smiled at her. "It's my pleasure, Dimi-tra."

"How do you do, Kýrie Angelis."

Nico found his place and sat. "Your name happens to be a particular favorite of mine."

"My mother's too. She's always loved the Greek myths and named me for the goddess of the grain."

Once upon a time Nico remembered an-other beautiful young woman who'd also loved the myths, but that had been in another world when he'd been a different person. "I've heard you have a remarkable mother and was told she would be here with you."

"Kyría Remis excused herself for a few minutes," Irena explained.

Melia brought his dinner and he started to eat. Dimitra looked across the table at him. "Kristos told me the Papadakis family wouldn't have made it through the last six months without you, Kýrie Angelis." Between her expectant light green eyes and warm smile, he could understand why Kristos was so taken with her.

"He's the best friend we could ever have!" Kristos blurted before Nico could get a word out. Kristos had just opened the gift Nico had given him—a framed picture of Tio when they'd first gone in the military. Tio had been eighteen and looked a lot like Kristos at that age. He showed it to Dimitra. "I'll treasure this, Uncle Nico."

"I've long wanted you to have it."

Kristos passed it to his mother, but at this point Nico looked beyond Irena to a woman of medium height who'd come out on the patio. A blue-on-white print dress clung to her stunning figure. Light from the candles illuminated the gold strands in her shoulder-length chestnut hair.

Only one woman he'd ever known had hair that color, but it had cascaded down her back like a mermaid's. Maybe he was hallucinating. He got to his feet and found himself looking into the sea-green eyes of the Aegean enchantress who'd stolen his heart.

Thee mou! he cried inwardly as she sat. It was *Mara*!

She looked to be in her late twenties, not the thirty-six she must be now.

Dimitra was *her* daughter?

Nico's mind reeled. As he did the math, he felt a stabbing pain in his heart. She'd told him she'd come to Salonica on vacation from France to be with her cousin. She must have been with another guy during the hours when he'd been at work for his father. She would have had the time to meet someone else. He smothered a groan. So many lies…

That was why she'd sent back all Nico's letters without reading them. She'd fallen for the other guy and had ended up having his baby. How many guys had she played while on vacation?

"Uncle Nico? Please meet Alexa Remis, Dimitra's mother."

Alexa? Since when?

It amazed him that Mara Tito, who'd supposedly returned to France after her vacation was over, could look him straight in the eye without flinching…unless she'd developed a serious case of amnesia.

The last thing he wanted to do was ruin this evening for Kristos and the attractive young woman seated across the table from him. He would play Mara's game for now. After nineteen years, Nico could be patient until he got answers he'd assumed would never see the light of day in this lifetime. But soon there would be a reckoning.

"Kristos has been anxious for us to meet, Kyría Remis. He's told me you're teaching English at the university." His thoughts reeled while he stared at her. To think she was back here in Salonica. A professor. The mother of the young woman Kristos loved. Nico was incredulous.

"Yes. I'm on vacation now but will be starting a full load in the fall. Dimitra is taking classes this summer," she said in a quiet voice, at this point avoiding his eyes.

No doubt she was terrified he was going to expose her. He had every right to destroy her in front of all of them. The way she was trembling, he could tell she was waiting for him to unmask her.

What in the hell had happened to the supposedly guileless young woman he'd met years ago and instantly adored? How could he have been so wrong about her? "I've learned you've been living in Ottawa, Canada, since your daughter was born."

She nodded, still afraid to meet his gaze. So much for the fictional woman living in France. Canada was where she'd been all these years? Nico couldn't comprehend it, let alone the fact that he was seated a few feet from the woman he'd loved to distraction.

She was more gorgeous than she'd been at

seventeen, and she'd given birth to another man's baby. But there was no ring on her finger. Had she not loved the father of her baby either? It was possible, given she'd made up the fiction that they'd been unavoidably separated. Nico couldn't fathom any of it, especially the letters she'd never opened. The fact that she had sent them back to him to make certain he got the message she wasn't interested had exhibited a cruelty he hadn't known her capable of.

He sat back, studying her through narrowed lids. "Our university is fortunate to have a teacher of your talents who's fluent in English and Greek."

"I'm the one who's fortunate, Kýrie Angelis."

Nico eyed Dimitra. "Are you going to follow in your mother's footsteps and become a foreign-language teacher too?"

She shook her head. "I'm looking at a degree in orthopedic engineering. It develops therapies to treat musculoskeletal disease."

"What would make you choose a field like that?"

"My *papoú* has arthritis, but he's also afflicted by the disorder. I'd love it if I could do something to help others like him one day."

"I told you Dimitra was intelligent," Kristos interjected. "Her math skills are off the charts."

Nico smiled. "I'm impressed, Dimitra." He was touched by her love for the grandfather Nico had never known existed. But she had a long, hard road of studies ahead of her. To combine it with marriage at this stage wouldn't be easy. He flicked his glance to Mara. "You must be proud of your daughter."

"She's wonderful."

"Mama is wonderful too, Kýrie Angelis. I do wish I'd known my father, but I've been lucky to have my *papoú* all my life. He's brilliant and a sweetheart."

Nico got the feeling Dimitra was a sweetheart too. But he'd been fooled before and worried that one day Kristos could be hurt after falling under Dimitra's spell. "I understand your *papoú* became the ambassador for Greece in Ottawa a long time ago."

"All my life, actually. Mama and I lived with him and my great-grandmother Iris until she died. Then we moved back here."

"I guess there'd be no point in asking how you like living here in Salonica, Dimitra."

She blushed while Kristos chuckled.

Just then sixteen-year-old Yanni came out on the patio and kissed his mom. With Nico's emotions in total chaos, Yanni's appearance gave him the perfect excuse to leave. He needed to get out of there. "Take my place, Yanni."

"Hey, Uncle Nico."

"I'm sorry I have to cut this short. I've got to go back to the office to deal with a situation that will keep me there half the night."

"I wish you didn't have to go," Irena murmured, "but I understand."

No, she didn't. No one but Mara had any idea what he was feeling as he walked around to give Irena a kiss.

"Thank you for a delicious dinner. We'll

talk later," he whispered before glancing at her guests. "It was a pleasure to meet you, Dimitra, *Alexa*. Kristos is a lucky man."

Dimitra beamed. "Thank you, Kýrie Angelis. I feel lucky too."

Mara avoided his gaze.

"I'll see you out, Uncle Nico."

Kristos walked him through the mansion to the car. "What do you think?" he asked before Nico got in the driver's seat. Kristos was painfully in love and Nico could see why. There'd be no talking him out of it.

"She's an intelligent, charming young woman. I find nothing wrong with her." It was the truth. That was the problem. Only time would reveal what wasn't visible right now.

Like mother, like daughter? Mara hadn't wasted any time finding another man to enamor within those three weeks. Or maybe she'd slept with the other guy after Nico had boarded the plane for military service. She hadn't been scheduled to return to France for at least three more days. That had been her story.

Who knew what had really happened though? How could he trust anything she'd told him? Seeing her tonight looking more beautiful than he could have thought possible brought it all back.

"Then will you tell Mama that?"

"I'm sure your mother feels like I do, but we'll finish this discussion when I don't have an emergency." Right now he couldn't think.

Kristos squeezed his shoulder. "I love the picture of Papa. Thanks for coming, for everything."

"Anytime. You know that." He wondered if Mara would be guilt ridden enough tonight to admit to the others that she'd known Nico a long time ago. It would be fascinating to find out how long it took her before she couldn't keep her secret from them any longer. Surely she had to know he wouldn't keep quiet forever about something so earthshaking.

Nico got behind the wheel and started the car. He pulled around the white BMW parked in front of him, which must be Mara's...or Alexa's...or whatever name she'd chosen to go by in her life.

His anger growing, he wasn't worried about her swimming away. Not this time. After nineteen years he knew where to go for the truth. It was time to be enlightened by the woman who'd once entranced him. Her disappearance had sent him to hell for a long, long time.

CHAPTER THREE

"Mama?"

"Come in."

Dimitra tiptoed into Alexa's bedroom and sat on the side of the bed. "I know you got sick tonight. You went so pale at the dinner table, I was frightened. And you were so quiet on the way home, I think you need to see a doctor."

Alexa *did* need a doctor, but not the kind her daughter was talking about. The bell had tolled for her tonight and there wasn't a physician on earth who could help her. Years ago, when her grandparents had asked her if she could handle her silence, she'd said yes, never dreaming she'd see Nico again. The flesh-and-blood reality of him had sent her into shock for a second time tonight.

"The sickness is passing, honey. I'm going

to be okay, but it saddens me this happened while we were having such a good time."

"Kristos's mother was so kind and friendly. I really like her. What I hope is that his Uncle Nico liked me and approves of me. I know he's not really his uncle, but Kristos worships him and loves him almost as much as his own father."

"I'm sure he thought you were wonderful. Who wouldn't love you?"

"You say that because you're my mom. I happen to know his opinion will go a long way with Kristos."

Alexa's heart pounded. "What about you?" she ventured in a trembling voice. "Did *you* like Kýrie Angelis?" She had to know her daughter's instant reaction.

"Who wouldn't?" her daughter responded so fast, Alexa couldn't believe it. "He's awesome in every way, Mama. You know that little photo of my father you gave me years ago? It kind of reminds me of Kýrie Angelis. My father was dark and handsome too. I can see why you fell for him. I hope that doesn't bother you for me to talk about my father."

Oh, Dimitra. You have no idea what those words mean to me since you'll probably be meeting him again—knowing who he is this time—within the next twelve to twenty-four hours.

"Of course it doesn't, and I just wanted to say that Kristos comes from a lovely family, honey. I'll send his mother a thank-you note for inviting us."

"I will too, but I'm worried about you."

"I'll be all right." She patted her daughter's hand. But Alexa couldn't predict anything about the future. Tonight she'd seen a dangerous glint in Nico's midnight-brown eyes that let her know there'd be no avoiding him now. She hadn't seen the last of him.

At nineteen he'd been a man of integrity and it appeared he still was. During dinner tonight he hadn't disappointed her. Another man might have created an ugly scene she would never have been able to survive. Not Nico. After all these years of no news, to see her again and realize she'd had a daughter and had been living a different life, his anger would have reached its zenith.

But he'd been born a breed apart from other men. For the short time he'd been at the Papadakis mansion, he'd known how to expose some of her lies and sins of omission with such expertise, no one suspected anything. That explained one of the reasons why he'd been made the head of the Angelis empire.

"Can I get you anything, Mama?"

"No, thank you, honey. All I need is sleep. This stomachache will pass."

Dimitra got up from the bed. "I'll check on Papoú now."

"He'll like that if he's not already asleep."

Her daughter lingered for a moment longer. "Will you tell me one more thing?"

Alexa moaned inwardly. "I like Kristos and his mother very much." She knew it wasn't the full answer Dimitra wanted, but she didn't dare discuss things now. Tomorrow she would contact Nico. Very soon the world Dimitra had known was going to change.

Once her daughter learned that he was her father, there was no way to predict the outcome of anything, let alone a possible marriage.

"I'm sorry, but I'm tired, honey."

"I know."

"Can we talk tomorrow?"

"Of course. Good night, Mama." Her resigned daughter gave Alexa a kiss before leaving the bedroom.

Alexa turned out the light on the bedside table and lay there in the dark, dying inside over so many things, not the least of which was her visceral reaction to Nico.

When she'd seen him on the patio, she'd found herself as out of breath as that moment in the sea when they'd run into each other years ago. He still had the power to transform her world until nothing existed but him. Though she knew he was a married man, it made no difference. She was still attracted to him.

Right now she was terrified over what was

to come once she'd phoned Irena Papadakis for Nico's phone number. Since Irena would learn the truth, if she hadn't already, Alexa would have to take the risk to ask for her help in getting in touch with Nico. She'd phone her first thing in the morning.

After five minutes her anxiety drove her out of bed and she got up to get a drink of water. While she was coming out of the bathroom she heard the ding on her phone. Someone had sent her a text, probably Michalis Androu, the divorced Cypriot also on the faculty.

Two months ago he'd invited her for drinks. A month later he'd asked her to go to the opera with him. She liked him, but shouldn't have accepted a dinner date for this coming Friday. It would be the last time.

She walked over to the bedside table to look at her phone and almost collapsed when she saw who'd sent it. How had he found her phone number? Her body trembled as she sank down on the side of the bed to read it.

This text shouldn't come as a surprise. We have to talk. I'll meet you at Ravaisi's on the beach at seven tomorrow evening. If you don't come, I'll drive to your house and wait for you for as long as it takes. Nico.

Alexa's eyes closed tightly. She fell back. *Ravaisi's.*

They'd eaten fresh seafood on its veranda on Perea Beach their last evening before he'd left for the military. It had been a night like tonight. The moon had looked like a pale yellow globe, lighting the calm water of the Aegean. Later they'd swum to his cruiser anchored a little way offshore.

She'd clung to Nico's hand as he helped her up the ladder. Once on board, he'd led her down the stairs to the lower deck. He'd planned a surprise for her on their last night together. All Alexa had to do was follow. She loved him with every fiber of her heart and soul and would follow him to the ends of the earth.

Nico had pulled her inside the bedroom and locked the door.

A cry of sheer delight escaped her lips at the sight that greeted her. The room had been filled with lighted candles, dispersing a fragrant scent of orange blossoms. Her gaze gravitated to an urn full of glorious blue hydrangeas placed on the bedside table. A few days earlier she'd happened to mention they were her favorite flower. He'd remembered everything.

Nico, she whispered in awe. *I feel like I'm in a dream.*

You look like one. When I first saw you in the water three weeks ago, I thought you were a mermaid coming out of the foam.

She clung to his hard body. His words would always have the power to make her blush. *Would you believe me if I told you I thought you looked like the statue of the young Emperor Augustus in the Salonica Archaeological Museum?*

Agape mou.

After calling her his love, he'd picked her

up like a bride and carried her to the bed. *Let me love you*, he'd said urgently. *The thought of not seeing you for another year is more than I can bear.* Nico pulled her on the bed and began to devour her. That was the first time they'd made love, the magical night Dimitra had been conceived.

Breathtaking memories of that night so long ago brought the tears gushing. There'd be no sleep for her tonight. Alexa got off the bed to wash her face. Somehow she had to get through tomorrow knowing what awaited her on that beach.

"You're still here, Kýrie Angelis?"

Nico looked up at the night watchman who'd worked for his father. It was ten after six in the evening. "Sunday's the best time to get things done. No one else is around."

"I never saw anyone work so hard."

"How else to try and fill my father's shoes?"

"You already do that, *kýrie*."

"Don't I wish, but thank you, Gus. I'll be

gone from here shortly. Have a good evening."

As soon as the older man left, Nico took his private elevator to the apartment above the office. After Raisa's death, he'd sold their villa in Salonica and had bought the one on Sarti, near the town of Sithonia that he now called home.

When he had to be in town, however, he stayed here for convenience since his father hadn't used it for several years. Last night after seeing Mara at dinner he'd flown to Sithonia to get some needed items, then he'd returned to the office apartment. Work was always waiting for him. Today he'd settled down to stay busy. It was the only panacea to keep him from climbing the walls while he waited for tonight to come.

Mara hadn't sent a message to let him know she'd received his text, let alone confirmed that she planned to meet him. He didn't have any expectations where she was concerned, but it didn't matter.

Nico couldn't get used to the idea that her

real name was Alexa Remis, that she'd lived with her daughter and grandparents in Canada after leaving Salonica for good.

No wonder Nico had never been able to find her! To think of the hours, weeks and months he'd spent trying to track her down in Greece, then in France. Tio had helped him after his marriage to Irena, but there'd been no trace of Leia or the Vasilakis family either. Like Mara, they'd disappeared off the face of the earth.

For a long time he feared the worst—that she'd been kidnapped or killed—even though there'd been no news of any kind to support that theory. His parents, who'd tried to help him, tended to think the same thing. It haunted him until one day when Giannina said, *Have you ever thought she just doesn't want to be found? Maybe she met another guy after you left and didn't want to tell you. Maybe she felt trapped.*

He'd stared at his practical sister, so wise even though she was two years younger. *You really think that's the answer?*

I don't know. I like guys, but can't imagine being tied down to one until I'm at least twenty-five or twenty-six. Maybe not even then. But for you to spend your life looking for her when you could have any woman you wanted makes no sense.

If that's true, then she was a coward not to tell me goodbye.

Maybe not a coward, but a flirt who got in too deep and was too young and frightened to tell you the truth. I know it's easy for me to say, but I wouldn't waste another minute thinking about her.

After all these years, their conversation rang true as he headed for Perea Beach. Last night he'd learned for himself that his sister had been right. Mara *had* met another guy and had had his baby. She'd also given Nico a false name and background.

Had she operated that way with every guy she'd met back then? Maybe she'd been young like himself, but he still had a hard time imagining most girls that age were so deceitful.

He made his way to the beach. A white

BMW sat in one of the parking spaces at the side of the restaurant. He recognized it from the night before and was glad to see she had the guts to face him and he wouldn't have to track her down.

Grabbing his knapsack, he got out of the car and walked inside. The hostess greeted him warmly. *"Kalispéra, kýrie."* She smiled at him. "I've seen you on television. Welcome to our restaurant."

"Efharisto."

"Where would you like to sit?"

"I'm meeting someone whom I think is already here, but I don't see her."

"Then she might be on the veranda. Feel free to go out and look for her."

He took a deep breath and walked through the restaurant to the door leading to the veranda. Nico and Mara had eaten outside that last night he'd been in Salonica. When he saw her seated now at the same table as all those years before, his heart dropped to his feet. The possibility that she'd suffered amnesia could be stricken off his list.

He sat opposite her and put his knapsack on the chair next to him. The sun wouldn't set for another hour and a half. The rays brought out the fabulous coloring of her hair. *"Kalispéra*, Mara."

"Kalispéra," she half whispered. Tears glazed her eyes, making them a deeper green, like the sea in front of them. In a simple pink top and white skirt, she looked so damn beautiful it destroyed any peace of mind he'd tried to achieve since last evening.

"I wondered if a day might come when we'd meet again by chance," Nico said.

"You're not the only one," she confessed.

Nico's brows furrowed. "The difference is, the Mara I fell in love with always knew where my parents lived and could have found me anytime to tell me she'd had a change of heart."

A distressed expression crossed over her features. "That's true, and no one deserves the truth more than you." But before she could say anything else, a waiter approached.

"I couldn't eat anything, Nico. Just coffee."

Food was the last thing on Nico's mind. "Two coffees," he told the waiter who came right back with them.

Once they'd been served, Nico reached inside his knapsack and handed her the bag he pulled out of it. "These belong to you. They've stayed in a storage closet for nineteen years. Once I had a dream that I'd find you and learn what terrible thing must have happened, like kidnapping or worse, that prevented you from answering them."

She sat motionless.

"I'd hoped to find you so we could read them together. But that day never came and I forgot about them until last night when I saw you walk out on the patio."

Her hand shook as she lowered her coffee mug and looked inside the bag. An audible gasp escaped her lips and she pulled out one of the unopened letters. She studied the address on the front of the envelope, then pulled out another one.

"There are dozens of letters here!" she cried, sounding incredulous.

Her acting was phenomenal. There'd been no kidnapping or worse. He knew she'd received them and had sent them back unopened. "That's right. All of them addressed to Mara Tito at the Vasilakis residence in Salonica." He drank more coffee. "You'll notice the Return to Sender handwritten on the side." She couldn't deny what she'd done. The proof was in her hands.

Alexa's head reared, causing her shimmery chestnut hair to settle against her shoulders. Tears poured down her white cheeks. Her breakdown of emotion surprised him.

He broke the silence. "For a long time I wanted an answer to the question why, but I don't need it now. Last night I met your daughter. Clearly you got involved with another man while you were in Greece and had his baby. For what it's worth, I would say you've done a wonderful job of raising her."

He put some euros on the table and stood. "Thank you for meeting me. *Andio*, Kyría Remis."

"No—wait, Nico!"

He ignored her cry and walked away. Never again.

It shouldn't have surprised Alexa that he'd said goodbye and left with an abruptness that took her breath away. His fear that something terrible had happened to her years ago crushed her with fresh guilt. Tonight he'd thought he'd learned the whole truth and was anxious to get home to his wife.

When she could get a grip on her emotions, she put the letters back in the bag he'd given her and left the restaurant on legs that barely supported her. During the drive home she trembled like a leaf. To her relief, Phyllis told her Dimitra had gone out with Kristos. Alexa's grandfather had fallen asleep watching a soccer match on TV.

Thankful to be alone, she grabbed a letter opener from his desk and hurried to the bedroom. She undressed and got ready for bed. Before her daughter came home, she wanted to read the letters Nico had written and kept all these years. How amazing that he hadn't thrown them away a long time ago.

Once under the covers, she emptied the contents of the bag. After a search she found the first letter he'd written to her in his unique penmanship. It was dated on the day he'd left Salonica.

Oh, Nico, darling... She drowned in tears. *You really did send them.*

The Return to Sender bore Monika's distinct hand. Even though Monika had confessed what she'd done fifteen years ago Alexa was hit with a wave of fresh hurt. How could she have done something so treacherous?

Using the opener, Alexa pulled out the one-page letter. A gold ring fell on the bedspread. Her heart pounded so hard, she thought she was going to be sick.

Mara—beloved
I have to write this fast. We're on a bus headed for the airport. I'll post this before I get on the plane.

Do you have any idea how I'm feeling right now? After spending last night in your arms, I'll never be the same. Saying goodbye to you felt like a part of me was being torn away.

Please wear this ring. I had it engraved for you. It's our engaged-to-be-engaged ring.

The sobs kept coming. Alexa could hardly read what had been engraved on the inside: *Gia Pánta.* It meant forever. She slid it on her ring finger.

You should get this tomorrow. I'll write you every night.

In three days you'll be going back to your mom in France. I look forward to meeting her after I get home.

We're going to have one wonderful wedding because you're going to become my wife. I can't wait.

Be sure that Leia forwards my letters the second she gets them. I won't be able to live until I start getting your letters and you send me your address in France. You can write to the address on the envelope and I'll get it no matter where I am.

S'agapo, Mara. I love you. You complete my life. Don't let anything happen to you. I couldn't live without you now.
Yours forever,
Nico

Convulsing, Alexa took a long time before her tears ebbed and she was able to search for the second letter he'd written. She tried to read it, but she began crying anew and it was almost impossible.

Agapiménos—my beloved
Boot camp is everything you've ever heard about, but I can handle it because I know I'll get a letter from you at the end of every day, telling me everything you've been doing.

When you're back in France, you better not fall for one of those French guys.

Good news. I'm bunking with a guy named Tio Papadakis. Would you believe his family owns the Papadakis Shipping Lines in Salonica? We have so much in common, it's crazy.

He's writing a redheaded girl in Salonica. Her name is Irena and he's planning to marry her before our tour of duty is finished. They'll be going to the University of Salonica too. We'll all be in school together.

Having just met Irena, and being in Tio's home with his children, Alexa could hardly go on reading. It was too piercingly wonderful and painful at the same time. Her tears made the ink run. Nico's love of life, his love for her, all of it had been ripped away, depriving them of the joy of marriage, of being parents and raising their precious Dimitra together.

Suddenly she heard noise and realized her daughter had come home. Alexa hurriedly put all the letters back in the bag, and hid it on the floor at the side of the bed. Then she turned off the lamp and drew the covers over her. Tomorrow would come soon enough, changing their lives forever.

In the middle of the night she couldn't stand it any longer. After turning on the lamp, she spent the next five hours reading one love letter after the other. Finally she read the last one he'd sent at the end of December, four months after he'd left Salonica. It was so short, it devastated her.

Mara darling

After all this time I believe in my heart something unspeakable has happened to you. Something beyond your control. The woman I love and who loves me wouldn't do this to us without a reason.

I live for word from you or about you. My prayer is that somehow, some way, you'll read this letter and be able to get in touch with me by any means available.

I'll never give up. If this letter is returned to me and I'm still in the dark after my service is over, I'll come looking for you and never stop.

Love forever,

Nico

Alexa finally recovered enough to put all the letters back in the bag except the last one, then got out of bed. After a shower, she dressed for the day in jeans and a T-shirt. With his last letter tucked in her back pocket, she left the bedroom. Her watch said eight thirty. Her grandfather would be up. She'd talk to him until Dimitra awakened.

Carrying the bag, she found him in the kitchen eating the breakfast Phyllis had prepared. He looked up. "There you are! I thought you'd be up before now. You don't look well."

Alexa kissed his forehead. "I've been awake since three o'clock. These are the reason why." She showed him the bag with the letters.

He studied several, then squinted at her. "There's only one way you're in possession of them. You've seen Nico. So…the long silence has been broken."

She nodded. "It turns out Nico Angelis was the best friend of Tio Papadakis. Would you believe it? He showed up at the dinner Saturday night. When we got home later, I received a text to meet him at a restaurant on the beach last night. He came with these letters.

"To quote him, 'For a long time I wanted an answer to the question why, but I don't need it now. Last night I met your daughter. Clearly you got involved with another man while you were in Greece and had his baby. For what it's worth, I would say you've done a wonderful job of raising her.' Then he said goodbye before I could tell him anything."

Her grandfather looked sad. "So he's a gentleman to the end."

She nodded. "This morning I'm going to tell Dimitra."

"Tell me what?" Her daughter had just come into the kitchen. Alexa turned her head toward her. "That you don't want me to marry Kristos? Did the thought of my being too young make you so upset we had to leave the dinner early? Was that it?"

Alexa took a deep breath. "No, honey. What I have to tell you has nothing to do with you and Kristos. Please sit down and listen. I have news that's going to change your world."

"I don't understand."

"Of course you don't. The fact is, I told you a half-truth the first time you asked me about your daddy."

"What do you mean?"

This was it. "Your father and I *did* get unavoidably separated, but I could have contacted him through his parents. There are reasons why I didn't do that or why I didn't reveal his true name to you."

"Which is?"

"Nico Angelis."

Her daughter laughed. "Are you teasing me?"

Heaven help me. "Not at all."

Dimitra eyed her incredulously. "You don't mean *the* Nico Angelis who came to dinner the other night—"

"Yes, honey. You said Kýrie Angelis reminded you of the photo I gave you of your father. That's because it is him. It's a picture I took of him when I was seventeen while I was on vacation in Salonica. In a short three-week period Nico and I fell madly in love and planned to be married after he finished his military service. He'd promised to write to me, but he never did, and I never heard from him again."

Dimitra paled and finally sat on a chair.

"I discovered I was pregnant two months after he'd left Salonica and we'd moved to Canada. When you were old enough, I told you your daddy's name was Dino. That was done to protect your reputation, and the grandparents and Nico from gossip. The news would have brought scandal to his illustrious family and to your *papoú*."

Tears filled Dimitra's eyes. "Is this the truth, Papoú?"

"Yes, sweetheart."

Alexa sat by her. "To this day Nico still doesn't know he's your father."

"What?"

"I never told him. Though your *papoú* knew how to get in touch with Nico's parents and would have gotten word to him that he had a daughter, I'm the one who begged him to do nothing because I was convinced Nico had only been having fun with me and had lost interest after he'd left. Saturday night was the first time I've seen him in nineteen years."

"You're kidding! What happened? Why didn't you ever hear from him? How could he have been so horrible to you?"

Alexa loved Dimitra for coming to her defense. She took a deep breath. "He wasn't the one who was horrible. My friend Monika, the girl I was staying with, was jealous of our relationship. Once I returned to Nicosia, she sent back every letter he ever wrote. But it took four years before she confessed to me what she had done."

Her daughter shook her head, looking totally fragmented. "I don't believe it."

"They're in that bag right there, stamped and postmarked. Nico was my errand last night and he gave them to me. You're free to read them. You'll learn a lot about your wonderful father. I loved him heart and soul. There's no one like him." Alexa pulled his last letter out of her pocket and handed it to her. "When you read this, you'll see what a remarkable human being he really is. He never lost his faith in us."

Her daughter took it from her, then jumped up from the chair. "But this is outrageous! She actually intercepted your letters and sent them back to him unopened?"

"Yes."

"That's the most hideous thing I ever heard!" Dimitra cried. Tears gushed down her cheeks. "How could anyone do something that evil?"

"It was a very evil act, I agree. After her confession, I was beside myself and wanted Nico to know the truth, that he had a four-year-old daughter. But your *papoú* found out he'd just gotten married to a prominent woman from a family from Athens. It was the biggest society wedding of the year in

Greece. He was also rising in his career and the media focus on him was growing."

Dimitra let out a wounded cry. "Was that more important than his finding out he had a daughter?" Her pain-filled words rang in the room.

"I couldn't bear the thought of risking his happiness when he'd found love again. Your *papoú* wanted me to tell him, but I was afraid of ruining his life, so I stayed quiet. After seeing him on Saturday night, I had no choice but to tell you the truth, knowing you'll never be able to forgive me."

She shook her head, still in disbelief. "He didn't act like he knew you…"

"No. He saved me the horror of having to confess to something you never knew about in front of everyone. There's no more honorable man alive than your father and he still has to be told you're his daughter. I would have told him last night, but he left the restaurant too fast because he was so upset to think I'd lied to him. I plan to tell him today.

"He should be at work. Of course I can't

expect forgiveness from him either. Please don't tell Kristos any of this until I've had a chance to talk to Nico first. He needs to hear this from me."

The look of desolation in Dimitra's eyes would haunt her forever.

CHAPTER FOUR

NICO'S CALL TO the port authority in Izmir was the first item on his busy agenda. Once completed, his phone rang. It was his sister at the newspaper.

"I'm so glad you answered."

"How are things going?"

"They'd be a lot better if Uncle Ari didn't squelch my ideas and put me down in front of the others. Sometimes he's actually cruel to me."

Nico's brows furrowed. "I knew he wasn't happy about your promotion over him, but that's no excuse. Baba felt you deserved to become the managing editor. I've never known anyone who worked harder."

"Thanks for saying that, Nico. I'll have to find a way to get along with Ari. But on to a happier note, it's Mama's birthday on Friday night. Let's plan a surprise for her and Baba."

Since last night, Mara had been the only thing on his mind. He couldn't think of her as Alexa. Giannina's phone call had caught him off guard. "What sort of plans?"

"How about a small party with friends on the yacht?"

"Sounds good."

"Nico? You don't seem like yourself. What's going on?"

"Do you remember years ago when you told me my girlfriend had probably fallen for some other guy and that's why she shut me down?"

"That was a ghastly time for you. I didn't know if you'd ever recover."

His eyes shut tightly. "Saturday night I met her by accident and you were right. She did meet another guy that summer in Salonica and then she moved to Canada. Now she's back and she has an eighteen-year-old daughter."

"Whoa. If I recall, I told you she probably didn't want to get in too deep."

"Not with me anyway. The point is, your astute comments at the time gave me another perspective that helped me move on. Eventually I met Raisa."

"I'm glad if anything I said made a difference."

"It did, and I thought you'd like to know. Count me in for Friday and call me when you need help. We'll talk then about what's going on at your work and come up with an idea to ease the situation."

"You're on. Love you."

No sooner had he hung up than his phone rang again. Only a few people besides his family had his cell phone number. If it was Kristos or Irena, he might not get any work done.

He checked the caller ID. Alexa Remis.

Nico gripped the phone tighter, not wanting anything to do with her. Why was she calling? Last night he'd walked away for good. That chapter of his life was over. Again. Or so he'd thought. He'd have to speak to her now though, otherwise it would bother him so much he wouldn't be able to concentrate.

He answered. "Kyría Remis?" Nico still couldn't call her Alexa.

"Thank you for answering. I know you're busy and so I'll make this quick. I have information you need to be told about as soon as possible, but I can't tell you over the phone. I'll meet you in the garden at the Vlatadon Monastery any time you say. Come alone."

What information?

He gripped his phone tighter. If this had something serious to do with Kristos and her daughter, surely Irena would have called him instead. His brows met in a frown. Her words, plus her tone, told him she'd meant every word.

"I can meet you there in half an hour." He hadn't planned on taking a lunch break, but would make an exception this once. The sooner this was over, the better.

"Thank you. I'll see you there." She hung up.

After letting his secretary know he'd be

out of the office for an hour, he left in his car and headed up to Ano Poli in the traditional area of Salonica. The Byzantine church she referred to had been built on the spot with a fabulous view of the sea. The Apostle Paul was said to have spoken to the Thessalonians from that vantage point. Nico and Mara had taken a picnic up there, enthralled with the place and each other.

He parked near her white car. A busload of tourists arrived as he walked around the side of the monastery to the garden. She sat on a bench at the far end beneath a tree where they'd once eaten their picnic. The second she saw him, she stood. Today she wore an attractive light green skirt and blouse. *Face it*. She'd always looked fantastic in anything.

"Thank you for coming." She acted frightened, which he found strange. "I wanted you to be alone because of what I have to say. Last night you walked away before I could tell you news that will not only change your life, but also that of your wife. You'll know better than anyone how to tell her if that's what you choose."

What in the hell was she talking about? "My wife died eleven years ago."

He heard a gasp before the color left her face. She couldn't have faked that reaction or the way she sank back down on the bench, close to a faint. Maybe a minute passed before she spoke. "I'm so sorry. I had no idea…" Her haunted eyes lifted to his in pleading. "Nico… Dimitra is *our* daughter."

He couldn't have heard her correctly. "What did you say?"

"I thought of course you'd figured it out at Irena's, but I know now from what you said that it didn't occur to you."

His body broke out in a cold sweat.

"*You* are her father. I told Dimitra you were called by the nickname Dino to protect her reputation after she was born to an underage woman who wasn't married."

It couldn't be true, could it? Nico thought he must be losing his mind.

"I know we took precautions, but she was

conceived anyway. When she was born, I had your name written on her birth certificate. My grandparents watched me sign it. Here's the proof." She reached for her purse and pulled out the paper.

His mind reeled. Incredulous, he sat and took the authentic-looking stamped and sealed document from her trembling hand and read it.

Certificate of Live Birth
Montfort Hospital, Ottawa, Ontario, Canada
Stamped and dated May 14
Mother of child: Alexa Soriano Remis
Father of child: Nicholas Timon Angelis
Full name of child: Dimitra Angelis Remis
Signature of attending doctor, M. Viret

When he lifted his head, those moist sea-green eyes stared into his. A calm seemed to have come over her. "This morning our daughter heard for the first time that you are her father. After leaving her in a shell-shocked condition with my grandfather, I came directly to you. There was a reason I lied to you from the moment we collided in the sea. But that's not the real story."

He stood and paced for a minute, rubbing the back of his neck while he tried to clear his mind. "I left you pregnant—"

Her chin trembled. "Yes, but neither of us could have known at the time."

The incredible news had rendered him speechless.

"Nico, you remember the myth we talked about where Hera almost caught Zeus with a mistress named Io? He turned Io into a heifer to deceive her. Hera wasn't fooled. Driven by jealousy, she placed Io where the giant would always watch her so Io and Zeus could never be together."

"Of course," he whispered. Nico remembered every minute of their time together, the things they'd said and told each other. You didn't forget things like that. To think that all these years Alexa had been raising *their* daughter. He couldn't comprehend it.

She got up from the bench. "That myth is *our* story, Nico."

"What do you mean?"

"My fictional cousin Leia Vasilakis was in reality a friend I met in Nicosia while I lived there. Her family worked with my grand-father who was the ambassador on Cyprus then. He made all of us take fictional names while on vacation because of political unrest, fearing the enemy might use me for a target."

Nico listened, but he had a hard time taking it all in.

"Last evening you told me you thought something horrible had happened to me. That was my grandfather's fear when I went on vacation, that an enemy might try to take me hostage to force my grandfather's hand in some insidious way. Thus the fake name. But I was never taken hostage. The person who carried out the treachery was my own friend, Monika Gataki. You knew her as Leia."

What she was saying now had the ring of truth, leaving Nico dumbstruck.

"Her family asked me to spend my three-week vacation with them in Salonica. The second day we arrived, I met you. From that first moment, Monika was so consumed by jealousy over my relationship with you, she found a way to hurt us and returned every letter you wrote to me at her parents' address. Her revenge was as total as Hera's, destroying your life and mine."

With each veil dashed from his eyes, Nico struggled for breath. "How could anyone have been that spiteful?"

"I asked myself that same question." She swallowed hard. "I didn't know what she'd done until four years later when she phoned me out of guilt and told me the truth. I almost died with that revelation, knowing it was too late for us."

"Too late?"

"Yes. My grandfather made inquiries about you and found out you were just recently married."

Nico wheeled around. Anger raged inside him. "It's never too late to learn you're a father! Married or not, why in the hell didn't you tell me we had a child? In fact, why didn't you get in touch with me the second you knew you were pregnant?"

She edged away from him. "I knew you'd ask me these questions. But the reasoning of a seventeen-year-old girl who was intimidated by what Monika had told me about your family won't make any sense to you. I've known from the beginning that neither Dimitra or you will ever forgive me. I'm leaving it up to the two of you to do what you want now that you both know the truth."

In the next instant she ran past him and the tourists toward the parking area while he stood there with the birth certificate—his *daughter's* birth certificate—still clutched in his hand.

Alexa had done the unpardonable to Nico. The second she returned to the house, a sobbing Dimitra met her in the living room. Her daughter had gotten dressed and had been waiting for her. She held up one of the letters.

"I've been reading everything. This is his

first letter to you. He loved you, Mama. He really loved you! I don't know how Monika could have done that to you. But it's *your* lie I can't forgive. You could have gotten in touch with his family when you found out you were pregnant. They would have contacted him. He would have uncovered the mystery because he's that kind of man. All these years I could have had my father."

"Honey—"

"I'm leaving," she broke in. "Kristos phoned and is coming for me. My father has already told him what you confessed at the monastery. I don't know when I'll be back." She flew out the front door.

"Dimitra—"

"Let her go, Alexa. Give her time."

She turned to her grandfather. "I did it all wrong, Papoú."

"You did what you felt was best for everyone. But now you have another problem."

"I know. My penance will be to live with what I've done for the rest of my life."

"That too, but I just had a call from Kýrie

Angelis. He's coming by for you in…" he checked his watch "…twenty minutes."

She panicked. "I don't believe it."

"Why? Dimitra needed to go off and talk everything over with Kristos. That leaves Nico. You dropped your bombshell, now he needs to talk everything over with you. He's one of the most important men in Greece, a man who has been used to taking charge all his life and doesn't hesitate. That's why he's so successful."

Alexa shuddered. "I've told him everything."

"In one hour? You think?" Her grandfather laughed.

"I'm afraid of his anger."

"I don't blame you, but now you've opened the door."

"Because I've been forced."

"Your grandmother Iris has to be cheering. She'd hoped for this day long before she passed away."

"So have you, Papoú," she said in a broken voice.

"When he gets here, I want him to come in so I can shake his hand. He never stopped trying to do the honorable thing where you were concerned. These letters prove it."

"I—I need to freshen up," she stammered and hurried to the bathroom.

Alexa looked and felt like death. The doorbell rang while she finished putting on lipstick. She still had to give her hair a brushing. When she walked back to the living room, Phyllis had already let Nico inside.

He'd changed out of his business suit and wore casual pants with a white crewneck cotton sweater. Her breath caught at his virile, masculine appeal.

Nico darted Alexa a glance. "It's an honor and privilege to meet your grandfather." She caught no hint of anger in his voice just now. "Gavril Filo has given remarkable service to our country, but even more, he has helped you raise our daughter. For that I'll be eternally grateful."

Moved by his kind words to her *papoú*, she walked over to the wheelchair and slid an arm around her grandfather's shoulders. "After my parents died, he and my grandmother raised me too. No one will ever know what they mean to me."

"I can only imagine."

Her grandfather lifted his head. "I can only imagine how much you two need to talk, even if it should have happened nineteen years ago. You go on, honey. Phyllis is here." He patted Alexa's hand.

Tears slid down her cheeks. She hugged him hard. "There's no one like you. I'll be back soon."

She and Nico left the house. With a sense of déjà vu, he helped her into a new black Mercedes and walked around to get behind the wheel. "The only place we can talk without interruption is my cruiser. It's not the same one. After I returned from military service and couldn't find you, I traded it in for a new one. You're the only person who would understand why."

"I do," she whispered. "That was the most

wonderful night of my entire life." He'd said the same thing in his letter.

"And our beautiful daughter was the result."

"Yes." Her voice throbbed.

He drove them toward the pier where he'd docked his boat in the past. "She has traits that remind me of my sister Giannina, but now that I think about it, her smile is all yours."

Alexa bowed her head. "Whenever I look at her, I see you." She struggled for breath. "How you must despise me." Her voice shook.

"To be sure, my anger over Monika Gataki's malicious actions is white-hot. As for my feelings of anger, frustration, hurt and disappointment where you're concerned, I'm trying to sort them out. But my first instinct after you left the monastery was to phone Kristos with the truth.

"He wants his mother's blessing and mine to marry Dimitra before long. That dinner at Irena's was meant for me to meet her and her mother. Now that I've learned she's our daughter, I felt it necessary that he know everything immediately."

"I'm glad you did. She loves him very much and will turn to him for comfort. I'll be lucky if she ever speaks to me again."

Nico's silence told her he agreed, causing her to shiver.

When they reached the pier, she got out and walked along the dock to a sleek blue thirty-foot cruiser. He helped her aboard and undid the ropes. After tossing her a life jacket, he started the engine and moved them out at wake speed. She sat across from him. In another minute they took off for open water.

Before long he shut off the engine and lowered the anchor. A hot sun shone down on them. Nico got up and walked over to one of the padded benches. "Come over here and help me put all this together."

She moved to the other bench opposite him. "It started with Monika."

"First off, tell me why she was so jealous. I'm still trying to get my head around it."

"Oh, Nico…" She made a sound. "You'd have to be a woman to understand."

"Try me." Wanting answers, he hadn't slept since the dinner at the Papadakis mansion.

"It began the day you and I met. When I swam back to the beach, I told her I'd met a guy named Nico Angelis, and that he wanted me to go on a boat ride with him. I didn't want her to worry while I was gone. It surprised me when she immediately flew into a rage about you."

"In what way?"

"She said she'd seen you on the beach before and wondered that I hadn't remembered what she'd said about you, your prestigious background and elite friends. She said you came from one of the most powerful, influential families in Greece. Monika warned me you were a playboy with movie-star looks and told me I was a fool to fall for your ridiculous line about my looking like a mermaid."

He sucked in his breath. "That was no act. You looked and swam exactly like one."

"Unbeknownst to me, the fact that you'd

asked me to go on your cruiser did a lot of damage. I realize now it was jealousy because you'd never sought her out. Even though she was attractive, you hadn't noticed her, but you'd shown interest in me. She'd been so sure you were just playing with me.

"When you kept coming around for the next three weeks, it was too much for her. She taunted me endlessly, but I was so crazy in love with you, I didn't let it bother me or realize what was happening to her."

He grimaced and sat forward with hands clasped between his powerful legs. "You never said a word of this to me."

"At the time I didn't worry that she was so upset. That realization came later. It wouldn't have occurred to me to tell you. It would have sounded like I was bragging, that you preferred me to her. The last thing I would have wanted was for you to think me petty, or that I found pleasure in hurting her.

"To my horror, I underestimated the depth of a dangerous jealousy that would drive her to destroy us. I'm afraid I was too naive and insecure to realize what was going on."

Nico got up, trying to contain his rage over what Monika had done. "I'd met her several times at the house when I'd gone to pick you up. I hadn't realized the depth of her bitter jealousy. She'd seemed nice enough. What in heaven's name made her admit to her evil?"

"Her parents noticed that she and I had stopped writing to each other. They were concerned and wanted to know why. For a long time she refused to tell them, and they knew something was terribly wrong. One day they broke her down and she confessed to returning the letters.

"They were horrified and called me to apologize. I'd always liked the Gataki family. They'd been kind to me and my grandparents. Monika got on the phone and cried. She said she knew I could never forgive her. I told her that was up to God."

Mara's character hadn't changed after all. His eyes played over her. "Did she know about Dimitra?"

"No. I never told her or her parents in the first place because I didn't learn I was pregnant until after we'd moved to Canada. Before her attack of conscience, if she'd known I was carrying your child, she likely would have gloated over my pain at being dumped, as she called it. I could imagine her calling me an idiot for believing that you loved me. I couldn't have withstood her mockery. That phone call from her and her family made me realize she did have a conscience, but she found it too late for us."

"I had no idea she would go that far," he ground out.

"No one did. After she confessed, I was afraid to call you with the news, knowing you'd recently been married to one of the most prominent women in Athens and had risen in the company."

Nico groaned aloud. "But letting me know I was a father the second you knew you were pregnant should have superseded every consideration!"

She shuddered. "You're right. It should

have, which proves I was a flawed human being not to get word to you from that first moment. And there's no excuse for not telling you the truth once I heard what Monika had done. My only defense is that I felt it would have been so cruel to tell you and your wife about Dimitra. It terrified me it could do real damage to your happiness.

"I tried putting myself in your place, Nico. Thinking about being newly married, how hard it would have been to suddenly hear you had a four-year-old daughter on the other side of the world. No bride would want to be told news like that. Not when she loved you and wanted to make a home and life with you, give you children."

Nico shook his head. Raisa had known how deeply in love he'd been with Mara. He agreed that to find out his former lover was alive and taking care of their four-year-old daughter so soon after his marriage to Raisa would have caused tremendous turmoil.

Though he imagined they would have stayed married, how did he know if Raisa could have handled his having a daughter from the woman he'd loved so desperately? The woman who was alive and had never married?

Again his lingering guilt over not loving Raisa as deeply as he'd loved Mara merged with his guilt that he hadn't been able to save her or their unborn child in that crash. That guilt would always torment him.

"You have to understand, Nico," she continued, unaware of his torment. "I didn't know if you would have welcomed a relationship with Dimitra at any age. The last time I saw you, you had to go off to do your military duty. You took my very soul with you. On our last night together you crushed me in your arms, promising to write me the second you could.

"But no letters had come by the time I'd returned to Nicosia with Leia's family four days later. After a week of being with my grandparents again, there still weren't any letters from you sent to me at her parents' house. You never phoned." Tears poured down her cheeks.

He grimaced. "Because I was in the military, the rules forbade me to make any phone calls. To think Leia intercepted all my letters and sent them back to me unopened... The pain she caused both of us was beyond cruelty."

Alexa nodded. "Her jealousy destroyed our dreams, knowing we were wildly in love. I remember waiting for Monika to call me and tell me the mail had come. My plan was to go over to her house and pick up all the letters I knew you would have sent me and forwarded."

Nico paced the deck. "How could that Monika have done such a thing?"

"It's beyond my comprehension. I waited and waited. There was so much I had to tell you, and I'd taken all those pictures I'd promised to send you. But in the middle of that nightmare, my grandfather received news that he'd been made the Greek ambassador to Canada. We were forced to leave immediately for his new post."

Another groan came out of Nico. "I can't believe you ended up in Canada."

"I about died having to fly so far away from you. Once we made the flight and had gotten settled in Ottawa, there were still no letters from you forwarded by Monika. At first I was convinced you'd been injured on maneuvers and couldn't write. After a month with no word, I knew something horrible must have happened to you. But if you'd died, it would have been all over the news. My grandfather assured me of that. Not hearing from you caused me the most excruciating pain I've ever known in my life."

"All because of Monika," he bit out.

"Yes. In time I finally had to accept the fact that Monika had been right. You'd played me, nothing more. It didn't seem possible, not after we'd planned to be married once you returned from military service. We'd dreamed of a whole life together and talked about children, but I decided you really hadn't meant it."

Nico looked out over the water, turned inside out by what she was telling him. "My letters proved otherwise."

"They did, but back then I had no knowledge of anything, and my agony increased when I discovered I was pregnant. I'd been nauseated at school and the doctor ran tests. I was so thrilled to be having your baby, but the unexpected news changed my entire world."

"It would have changed mine if you'd gotten word to my parents."

"I realize that now. My grandfather said he would track you down through your family so you could know you were a father. But I begged him not to do anything.

"I remembered you telling me your family had been forced to live down a scandal to do with your uncle Ari. I couldn't remember details, but you said it had affected your aunt in a terrible way and she'd never been the same. I didn't want to add to that misery with another scandal. And I felt such shame that my time with you had been nothing more than a summer fling, the kind Monika had alluded to."

Nico let loose a curse.

"My only excuse was that I was a witless teenager who'd ignored my grandparents' advice and had gotten into trouble like so many other girls. I definitely didn't tell Monika I was expecting. She would have derided me for being the gullible fool who would now pay the price forever. I chose to say nothing to avoid her merciless ridicule."

He lifted his head to look at her. "What's happened to Monika?"

"Over time we stopped writing letters. She never had faith in your love for me. I no longer considered her a friend by the time she told me the truth. The last contact with her was that phone call. It altered my view of life."

"Tell me about it," he said in a withering tone.

"I've gone over that moment for nineteen years. What if I'd told Monika I was pregnant the moment I knew? Would she have felt shame and admitted to me what she'd done to sabotage our love? Would she have confessed that she'd returned every letter? Or would she have laughed and stayed silent?"

"That was a missed opportunity."

"It was, Nico, and I'll suffer for it for the rest of my life. Last month I saw you on TV and it made it worse to know you were so close."

"You saw me on the news?"

"I've seen you several times, and it has haunted me. I reasoned that Dimitra was an adult now and could make up her own mind if she wanted to get to know you. Her age and distance were no longer a problem for visits.

"But I worried about you. Would you welcome a relationship with your grown-up daughter at this stage of life? How would it affect you and your wife and children? I was tortured by endless questions with no satisfactory answers. Then I saw you at Irena's…"

"You handled your shock well enough," he muttered.

"Thank you for not exposing me in front of the others. Dimitra will always blame me for keeping her apart from you. I know she'll never forgive me. I don't deserve forgiveness and will never know the answer to certain questions if I'd just come forward with the truth.

"Naturally you would have had no choice but to think the worst about the girl who'd promised to write you back faithfully every day until your military duty came to an end."

Nico couldn't take much more of this.

"I was blessed to be able to turn to my patient, loving grandparents who listened to my heartfelt plea to stay quiet and honored my wishes. They agreed to help me raise my love child. It wasn't fair to them, Nico. They raised me from the age of five when my parents were killed in a train accident. My grandparents were and are saints."

"I agree."

"As you can imagine, Dimitra has turned out to be the great joy of my grandparents' lives. She's also my darling daughter who became my raison d'être."

CHAPTER FIVE

Alexa walked around the deck for a minute, then drew closer to Nico. "Would you tell me a bit about your wife? Were you happy with her, Nico? Tell me you were."

"Yes." It was the truth.

"I'm so glad. It means you recovered from what happened with us and wanted love in your life again."

He gripped the side of the boat. This conversation about Raisa needed to end. "Didn't you?" he riposted. "I can't imagine your not finding someone else."

"There were two men I cared about in Canada, but I could never be sure how Dimitra would be able to accept one into our lives."

"Then you did entertain the idea."

"Yes, but I could never commit. Dimitra has always been my priority. Close as I came to marriage in the past, I was afraid to go through with it in case it didn't work out and she was unhappy. I'd rather have seen her future settled first, whenever that time came.

"Then she met Kristos. I know her love for him is real, but they're still so young. I'd rather they waited another year at least. As you and I have learned, you never know how long love will last, no matter the reason for it getting cut off by unforeseen circumstances."

Nico had been the victim of unforeseen circumstances twice in his life. "It's Irena's fear too." He looked out over the water, still incredulous over what he'd learned.

"Do you mind if I ask how you met your wife? Unless it's too painful."

"Not at all." He turned so he could look at her. "I learned to fly in the military, but that was after I stopped sending you letters. When I returned home I bought a small plane. I soon started flying everywhere when I had to go to meetings outside of Salonica. One evening I flew to Athens and met Raisa at a party for a friend.

"We started talking and one thing led to another. It felt good to connect with someone again and we began seeing each other on a regular basis. I thought it would put her off when I told her about you and me. She knew I was still looking for you, but she was patient and never gave up. The day came when I realized my search was futile. That's when I asked her to marry me.

"One morning I took her on a flight with me and a coworker. She'd just found out we were expecting. It was a beautiful clear day with a nice tailwind. But then, suddenly, our flight from Chios where we'd celebrated our exciting news took on a different dimension.

"I had to struggle to keep us straight and level. In a flash, up became down. It was wind shear. Our seat belts barely restrained us. We crashed. I and my coworker survived, but Raisa didn't make it. I haven't taken control of a plane since."

Alexa moved closer. "You lost your wife and unborn child. Oh, Nico. I'm so heartsick for you, I don't know what to say." The compassion in her voice sounded like the old Mara, calling up memories.

"That was eleven years ago. Since then I've immersed myself in work. To learn I have a daughter is a miracle I never expected. I don't know if she'll want a relationship with me, but I plan to find out."

"More than anything in this world I want the two of you to have one."

His breath caught. *Why? To placate your guilt?* Nico had listened to her reasons for keeping silent. On an intellectual level, he understood. But it didn't erase the pain. He couldn't talk about this any longer. "I'll take you back home before your grandfather starts to worry."

They went back to the pier and he drove her home in silence. En route she turned to him. "Nico? I promise you that our daughter has wanted her father all her life. I gave her a small photo of you when she was around five which she has treasured. It was your profile. When we got home from Irena's, she said you reminded her of the picture I gave her.

She also said you were awesome. Now that she knows you are her father, her world has been transformed."

"You can't know that when she's only just learned the truth," he bit out.

"But I do. Not only does she adore Kristos who adores you, Dimitra read your letters after I left for the monastery. She's already your champion. When I returned, she said, 'He really loved you, Mama. I don't know how Monika could have done that to you, but it's *your* lie I can't forgive. *You* could have gotten in touch with his family as soon as you found out you were pregnant. They would have contacted him and he would have uncovered the mystery because he's that kind of wonderful man.'"

Though Alexa's words about Dimitra worked like a balm on Nico's tormented soul, they didn't take away the remembered pain of those dreadful first years. Being with Mara, talking with her like this, had opened a deep wound.

Every explanation she'd given him for her

silence had expressed fear of hurting him or bringing shame to him and their families. The sweetness he'd found in her from the start was still an inherent part of her nature. He could never blame her for wanting to avoid causing his family pain.

After hearing her explanations, he could see how difficult everything had been for her. But he couldn't help thinking that one phone call nineteen years ago, after she discovered she was pregnant, would have made their lives so different.

When they reached the house, she got out. "I'll run inside. In case Dimitra is there, shall I send her out?"

"I don't want to force something on her she's not ready for. I'd prefer to phone her and we'll go from there."

"All right."

"Alexa?" He couldn't believe he had to call her that now.

"Yes?"

He paused for a moment, but he was too full of emotions to say anything more right now. "Nothing. It'll keep."

She whispered good-night and hurried into the house.

With a groan, he phoned Irena.

"Nico?"

"Sorry to call this late. Is Kristos home by any chance?"

"No. He's still out with Dimitra. I thought I'd better let you know her mother called to ask me for your phone number. I admit I was surprised."

Nico sucked in his breath. "I'll tell you why after I speak with him tomorrow." He couldn't go into it now.

"You don't sound yourself."

His hands tightened on the steering wheel. "I'm not. I'll explain later. *Kalinikta*, Irena."

After hanging up, he left for headquarters and sent Kristos a text.

Call me before you go to bed. I don't care how late.

He'd barely entered his office when his phone rang and he answered immediately. It was Kristos. "Thanks for calling me."

"I would have phoned you without your text, Uncle Nico. Dimitra is still with me and wants to talk to you, but she doesn't know how you feel now that you've been told the truth."

His throat swelled with emotion. "I'm over-joyed to learn I have a daughter." As he'd told Alexa, Dimitra was a miracle.

"I knew it! And that's exactly how she feels about you. Where are you?"

"At my office."

"Can we come over? She doesn't want to wait any longer to talk to you."

Neither did Nico, who was only now begin-ning to unthaw and realize he had a daughter. "I'll tell Gus to let you in."

"We'll be there in five minutes."

It was the longest five minutes Nico had ever lived through and he stood by the el-evator, waiting anxiously. When the doors opened, Dimitra emerged. She'd come up alone with a tearstained face.

"All my life I've wished I could meet my father. To think we've already had dinner together and you've always been here. I just didn't know it." Her voice trembled. "Do you mind if I call you Baba?"

"I'd be crushed if you didn't." Nico held out his arms and she ran into them. *I kóri mou. My daughter.* He was holding the child he and Alexa had created. It didn't seem possible. He rocked her for a long time, overwhelmed that this blessing had come into his life...a life he'd thought had lost its flavor forever.

This loving young woman had been the product of a great love. Raw anger rose inside him for the years he'd missed being a father to her.

He knew and understood why Alexa had done this to them, but it still hurt to the core of his being.

The next Friday night after dinner with Michalis Androu—whom she'd politely told she wasn't ready to explore a relationship—Alexa went in the house, torn apart by all that was happening. The last time she'd been with

Nico, the solemn side of him was so different from the man Alexa had fallen in love with, she found herself mourning for the old dynamic Nico. He'd been a man full of life and had made her thankful to be alive.

She kissed her grandfather good-night and went to bed. Since the night her daughter had gone off with Kristos, Dimitra had treated her like a stranger. For the last five days Kristos had picked her up and brought her home from the university before he went to work but Alexa hadn't seen or talked to either of them.

On Saturday morning Alexa awakened early, put on her headphones and left to go for a run around the neighborhood while Dimitra was still asleep. The only thing that helped relieve stress for Alexa was to get out of the house and run for a half hour every morning. She'd been doing it for years.

It wasn't until she got home and removed the headphones that she saw she'd received a text.

Nico.

Would the day ever come when her heart didn't jump at the sight or sound of him?

She sank down on the bed to read it.

Can you come to my office ASAP? I'll inform the front desk to send you up in the private elevator. This is important.

Alexa put a hand to her throat. Naturally it was important where their daughter was concerned. In a week his whole life had been turned upside down. So had hers. She answered him.

I'll be there in an hour.

After a quick shower, she dressed and told her grandfather she'd be back soon. Dimitra still hadn't come out of her bedroom when Alexa left for Angelis headquarters.

The fact that Nico was now CEO of a huge conglomerate hadn't escaped her. But at seventeen she hadn't truly realized what his destiny would be. She pulled into the guest parking and walked inside. After introducing herself, the male receptionist escorted her to a private elevator and pressed the button that sent her skyward.

Once the doors opened, Nico stood there wearing white cargo pants and a dark blue polo shirt. He'd always loved casual clothes and had staggering appeal no matter what he wore. Their eyes fused for a moment, taking her back in time to that first moment in the Aegean. She'd thought him drop-dead gorgeous at nineteen. He'd only grown more attractive over the years. Nico had exceeded the promise of the breathtaking man in the teenager.

"Thanks for coming."

"I'm glad you texted me. Our daughter isn't speaking to me, but I know she's been with you this week. I hope you can tell me how she's handling things." She followed him into his large, impressive office that matched a man of his stature and importance.

He indicated the couch for her to sit, then found himself a chair. "I thought you should know that last evening I took her to meet her aunt and grandparents. It was Mama's birthday and we had a party on the yacht. Giannina arranged everything. Dimitra has brought them the greatest happiness they've ever known."

"You've done the same thing for her, Nico." Despite the anger he had to feel for what Alexa had done, he'd embraced their daughter and had welcomed her into his family. Alexa had loved him heart and soul years ago. Now she loved and adored him more for the loving father he'd become just knowing of their daughter's existence.

"It's especially touching for them since she's their only living grandchild. I wanted you to know they've welcomed her with open arms."

Marvelous as the news was, Alexa jumped up, too anxiety ridden over her own guilt to sit still. She hugged her arms to her waist. "Dimitra has to be overjoyed to find the missing piece of her life and be accepted so completely. But I can only imagine what they think of me."

"They know everything." He stood. "When you went missing, they tried to help me find you."

Alexa hadn't known that. Her silence had touched his family too. Her heart hung heavy for Nico. If his wife hadn't died, there would be two grandchildren for his parents to love.

"I'm touched that they tried to help you. It's all the more reason why they must despise me for what I've done to you and Dimitra."

"For now they're reserving judgment because they're too happy. But there's something you need to know. A press release will be coming out in the media. I didn't want you to find that out before I told you. It's going to affect all of us and the people we associate with, including Raisa's parents and siblings."

Alexa's hand went to her mouth. "The news is going to be so hurtful for them."

"They knew about you."

"But not our daughter, who might never get past what I've done."

His piercing dark gaze found hers. "One

thing I've learned since the dinner at Irena's. Don't ever say never."

She took a deep breath. "You're right. I never thought I'd see you again and here we are."

He grimaced. "It was like that moment when you swam back to me at Perea Beach. I feared you were a mermaid who'd disappeared on me and was gone forever until you cried my name. Nineteen years later you appeared once more, this time on Irena's patio."

She took a deep breath. "Fate had a way of uniting you with Dimitra. I'm reminded of the Greek myth about the three Fate goddesses who assigned individual destinies to mortals at birth.

"Lachesis, the Alloter, kept all knowledge of Dimitra from you. Yet even Lachesis's power couldn't prevent you and Dimitra from meeting." She cleared her throat. "We have Kristos to thank for that. Maybe it *is* true love between them, and it's so powerful it broke the spell."

"Maybe," he murmured, putting a hand on

her arm. His touch sent darts of awareness through her body. "Your knowledge of the myths is remarkable."

Little did he know Alexa had made them a lifelong study. She lifted her head. They were so close, she could imagine him kissing her and wanted it so badly she could taste it.

"Nico, thank you for telling me about the party. For Dimitra to be accepted and loved by you and your family will have made her feel reborn. As for being forewarned that there'll be a media explosion, I'm now fore-armed. I can't thank you enough. Now I have to get back to my grandfather and will let myself out."

For self-preservation she had to get out of there. Being with him like this was the hardest thing on earth to handle. He ran a hand up her arm before letting her go. The old Nico wouldn't have let her walk out of there.

As she rode the elevator to the lobby, she had to admit that all these years apart hadn't changed her feelings for Nico. If anything, they'd grown stronger. Just now she'd wanted to throw herself in his arms the way she'd done years ago while they'd kissed each other senseless.

But the myth about Hera and her jealousy of Io had done its damage, and Alexa had made it worse by keeping quiet. The result had caused her to lose Nico as she'd known it would if he ever learned the truth. If there'd been a glimmer of hope that deep down he still wanted to be with her, he would have pulled her back so she couldn't leave his office.

As she walked to her car, she was left with one heart-wrenching, undeniable truth. *You'll always be in love with him.*

Nico watched the elevator doors close.

A primordial urge to go after her shook him to the core. The desire for her that had burned nineteen years ago blazed hotter than ever. All the pain he'd lived through hadn't extinguished it. Knowing what she'd done to keep the knowledge of their child from him, hearing her reasons why, still hadn't killed his longing to be with her. How was that even possible?

Yet she'd left his office as soon as he'd told her about the family party and how the news he had a daughter would get out and impact all their lives. The Mara he'd loved would have stayed and ended up in his arms. But he had to get it in his head that she'd grown up and changed. There was no Mara. She'd turned into Alexa.

This was one time when he needed Tio—the one person who'd been there at the height of Nico's pain and could understand what seeing Alexa again, now, meant to him. Only his best friend could know what Nico was going through right now and would tell him this insanity would pass. But would it?

Dimitra was a constant reminder of her mother. The thought that he'd never be free of his memories was so terrifying, he rushed over to the desk and buzzed his secretary to tell him that he was leaving. Irena had become his best friend. He'd drive over and talk to her about how he could have a relationship with his daughter that didn't include Alexa.

But a half hour later, his talk with Irena on the patio brought no relief.

"Kristos has told me how much Dimitra already loves you, Nico. But she also adores her mother, even if she's in turmoil right now. You and Alexa are her parents, and you're both going to be included in her life from now on. The sooner you can handle that the better because… I have news. I would have called you if you hadn't come over."

Nico didn't like the sound of more news and got to his feet.

Irena eyed him with compassion. "Kristos gave her a ring last night."

He stopped pacing. "Somehow that doesn't surprise me. He loves her. Now that her circumstances have changed, he wants to protect the woman he loves."

"I agree. So it's up to you and me how we accept the news, even if we still believe it's too soon. My father-in-law will erupt when he hears."

"If I know your son, he won't care and wants to shout it to the world." Nico had felt the same way about Mara.

She nodded. "He already asked me if we could have an engagement party here, but I told him nothing could be done without her mother being involved."

Nico rubbed his lower lip with his thumb. "I was with Alexa at my office earlier. She doesn't think Dimitra will forgive her for what she did. But what you've just told me has given me an idea. Do you know Kristos's schedule for today?"

"Only that he was picking up Dimitra and probably wouldn't be home until late."

"Good. That might give me time to tell Alexa the latest news and plan a strategy that will help mother and daughter work through their pain."

"If anyone can bring that about, it's you, Nico. But what about *your* pain?"

"Like you said, the sooner I can handle

the fact that Alexa and I are both inextricably involved in our daughter's life, the better. Thanks for talking to me, Irena. You've been a big help. Now I've got a phone call to make and will tell you the outcome later."

He kissed her cheek and let himself out to make the call. Maybe Alexa didn't want to hear from him so soon, but a part of him rejoiced that he had a vital reason to talk to her before the day was out. What was wrong with him? Where was his loyalty to Raisa to even be thinking this way?

After picking up some groceries, Alexa drove home filled with anxiety. Dimitra still wasn't speaking to her, and she couldn't bear it. After seeing Nico and hearing about his family party, she wanted to connect with her daughter and know how she was feeling about her new family. So far, Nico had been Alexa's only conduit for information.

Once in the house, she realized no one was home. Phyllis had probably taken her grandfather out on this beautiful day. Dimitra had to be off with Kristos. Alexa put the groceries away, remembering those moments in Nico's office when she would have given anything for him to pull her into his arms. How insane was that? As if her thoughts had conjured him, her phone rang and she saw the caller ID.

Her heart leaped to her throat before she answered it, struggling to sound normal. "Nico?"

"Have you heard the news?" he asked without preamble.

She trembled. "I don't know what you mean."

"That's good. Do you have plans for the rest of the day?"

"Nico…don't keep me in suspense."

"We have to talk, but not on the phone."

This had something to do with Dimitra she wasn't going to like. Maybe she was planning to move out because she couldn't stand to be around her mother anymore. "I'll meet you wherever you say." She felt desperate.

"Why don't I come by for you? How soon can you be ready?"

Her eyes closed tightly. This was serious. "Right now." It was close to four o'clock.

"Then I'll be there in ten minutes."

She clicked off and freshened up in the bathroom. Makeup would help put some color in her cheeks. With a coat of coral lipstick and a quick brushing of her hair, she felt a little more presentable. Not that Nico would notice. What an irony that the man she'd turned into an enemy was turning out to be the only person she could appeal to for help. Nothing was making sense right now.

CHAPTER SIX

AFTER LEAVING A NOTE on the fridge saying that Alexa was with Nico and would be back later, she walked out to the curb in front to wait for him. The sight of the black car and striking male driving it shouldn't have excited her. The way she was feeling, she could be seventeen again. Once the car came to a stop, she got in before he could walk around and open her door for her.

Their gazes collided. "If the news is bad, please drive us somewhere away from the house. I don't want Dimitra or my grandfather to come home and see me too upset to face them."

He started the car and they took off. "I thought we'd drive to Pella and enjoy the Roditis wine you used to love."

She panicked. "You think I'm going to need

it?" He'd taken her there one glorious day long ago. They'd been delirious with love while they sampled the pink wine from a vineyard under a hot sun.

"I think we both do."

Alexa fastened her seat belt, not knowing how to deal with that remark. "Why didn't you just tell me what this is about before I left you earlier?"

Nico drove with a mastery that was reflected in everything he did. "I left the office right after you did, but I didn't hear the news until I dropped by Irena's. Kristos and our daughter got engaged last night."

The news wasn't what Alexa had expected. She was so surprised, she didn't say anything at first.

"What's made you go quiet?"

She bit her lip. "I thought you were going to tell me that Dimitra was moving out. That's been my greatest fear." Her voice had started to wobble. "I thought she despised me so much she couldn't stand to live with me anymore. I wouldn't have blamed her. In fact I've had nightmares about it since I saw you at Irena's."

He reached out to cover her hand. His warmth enveloped her whole body. Nico could have no idea how much she craved his touch. "If you'd heard the marvelous things she'd said about you to my parents and Giannina, you'd know the thought has never crossed her mind."

Nico's words broke Alexa down and she sobbed. He held her hand a little tighter before letting it go.

"Thank you for being so kind to me, Nico." She wiped her eyes. "I don't deserve it after what I've done to you. In truth I don't know how you can stand to be around me."

She heard his sharp intake of breath. "This afternoon Irena reminded me that you and I will always be involved in our daughter's life. It will help all of us if we get along and do what's best for her. That's why I wanted you to come with me. Sharing Dimitra is a new experience for both of us. I'm trying to tread carefully."

"And doing a beautiful job of it!" she declared, lifting her head to look at him through tear-drenched eyes. "I mean it, Nico. Besides everything else, you really are an exceptional human being. Our daughter has already figured that out."

"Then let's decide what to do next. I believe you and I and Irena are all in agreement about Kristos and Dimitra moving too fast. But that ring on her finger has made it a fait accompli. It's my opinion that if the first thing we do as her parents is fight them on this engagement, then—"

"Then it would be the worst thing we could do," she broke in. "I couldn't agree with you more."

By now they'd reached the vineyard outside Pella. Nico slowed down and drove along the road to the winery. A few tourists came out the door. "What do you say we go in and plot."

For a moment he sounded just like the old Nico, filling her with thrill after thrill. She laughed all the way inside the winery's front door. It astonished her she could do that when she'd been sobbing so hard before. He found them a table and ordered the same wine they'd once enjoyed. "This is like a window in time for me," she said.

Over the rim of the wineglass his dark eyes stared at her with an intensity that made her quiver. "For me too. I haven't been back here since." His deep voice pierced her insides.

She sipped her wine, unable to believe they were together like this again. But it was dangerous to go down that road of the past. To break the spell he'd been casting on her since they'd been in the car, she changed the subject.

"I'm thinking something should be done to celebrate their engagement. If I show Dimitra I support her, maybe it would help our relationship."

He nodded. "You took the words out of my mouth. Since I'm a friend of the Papadakis family and would do this for Kristos and his mother no matter what, you and I could host an engagement party for them at my villa on Sarti. We'd let them make up the guest list."

Was there ever a more wonderful man born? Her eyes filled. "That's very generous of you, Nico."

"We're only talking an engagement party. Being the mother of the bride, you'll be the one to plan the wedding when the time comes. That is if they make it that far." When her face fell, he laughed.

"You're still a big tease." She was loving this time with him so much it frightened her. "Sometimes in the past you were so exasperating, I wanted to run away from you."

"But you didn't," he said in his deep voice, capturing her gaze. "Even if you'd tried, you know you wouldn't have gotten very far."

"You're right. I fell for you so hard, I would have turned around and flung myself at you. I was pathetic."

His devilish grin set her on fire. When they'd been on his cruiser together talking about everything, he'd been upset and morose. Today she saw no sign of that side of him, thank heaven. She couldn't bear it if he wasn't the same wonderful Nico she would always adore.

Nico's dark eyes played over her in the old familiar way that sent her heart thudding. "I'm glad to see a smile on your face." That was only possible because being with him again had brought her to life. He provided the magic. "If you're ready, we'll drive back to Salonica. When I take you home, we might run into the happy couple and can tell them what we'd like to do for them, if they're amenable."

"They'll be overjoyed and you know it. I could never deny you anything. Our daughter is no different."

"But you did deny me," he came back, surprising her.

"What do you mean?"

A mysterious look crossed over his handsome face. "Have you forgotten I asked you to run away with me after we finished our wine here years ago?"

She laughed. "But you weren't being serious."

"Oh, I was deadly serious. Remember that hot-air-balloon concession we passed that day? I'd planned for the person taking us up to head for Hellenia where my uncle's family lived. We could have hidden out there with no one the wiser and waited until you'd turned eighteen. Then we could have gotten married and started a new life."

"Nico—I don't believe it!"

"At the last minute I changed my mind because an even better plan came to me that wouldn't involve my uncle. But it would take a lot more planning."

She flashed him a wide smile. "Am I going to hear about that one?"

"One of these days when we're not pressed with helping our daughter, I'll share it all."

"I don't know if I want to hear it."

"Why not?"

"Because I'll wish you'd carried it out."

That deep, rich laughter burst out of him, filling her with joy. On the way back they

talked about possible dates for the engagement party. When he pulled in the driveway,
they didn't see Kristos's car.

"I imagine Dimitra is still out with Kristos." She opened the door, afraid to remain
any longer and realize she'd rather stay right
where she was and never leave. Before getting out she turned to him.

"No matter how this goes with our daughter, I'll never be able to thank you enough for
everything you've done to make this easier.
You never deserved what I did to you."

"We didn't deserve what Monika did. Why
don't we agree not to talk about that anymore.
That portion of our lives is over."

"You honestly mean it?"

"How could I not when I've been united
with our daughter. It's a time to rejoice, not
wallow in pain."

This sounded like the Nico she'd once loved.
"All right. We won't go over that ground anymore. Thank you for today. *Kalinikta*, Nico."

She dashed toward the house and hurried
inside, surprising her daughter and grandfa-

ther who sat talking in the living room. She was back after all!

Their *papoú* smiled. "We're glad you're home, Alexa."

Her daughter avoided acknowledging her.

"I couldn't get here soon enough." She moved closer. "I've just heard you're engaged to Kristos."

Dimitra jumped up looking shocked. "You already know?"

"Yes. Irena told your father and he just told me."

"If you're going to tell me we're too young to—"

"I'm not," Alexa interrupted her. This was the first time her daughter had said a word to her in days. "We both think you and Kristos are perfect for each other."

Her eyes lit up. "You mean it?" she cried.

"With all my heart."

"My father thinks so too?"

"Yes. He thinks *you're* perfect and will make Kristos a wonderful wife. So do I. As you reminded me a week ago, I told you I met the one at seventeen. Now it's your turn, and you're *eighteen*."

"Mama—" Her daughter reached for her and they hugged. Alexa's grandfather had tears in his eyes, smiling his approval.

"Your father has offered his villa on Sarti to announce your engagement. He's asked me to help him. But only if it's what the two of you want."

A cry of pure joy came out of her. "We couldn't want anything more! All my dreams are coming true!" She hugged her *papoú* hard, then turned to Alexa and hugged her again. "I've got to phone Kristos and tell him what's happened."

After she disappeared, Alexa's grandfather shared a long glance with her. "You made a very wise decision just now."

"Don't give me too much credit. That's Nico's influence. He knows more about parenting than I do."

"I disagree. You've been a wonderful mother, otherwise Dimitra wouldn't be making this kind of progress so fast."

"You're the wise one and I'll love you for-ever." She reached out and put her arms around him. Alexa wasn't naive enough to think everything was perfect, but at least the three of them were functioning enough to get through this first stage. For that blessing she was beyond thankful.

Two weeks later, after college classes were over on Friday, Nico drove Alexa, Dimitra and their *papoú* to Sarti. He could have ar-ranged for them to fly to Sithonia and then go on to Sarti, but the scenery was worth the drive. His daughter sat up front with him. Alexa got in the back to help her grandfather during the eighty-plus mile ride. They would stay at his villa for the weekend.

Kristos was coming by helicopter. The party would take place on Saturday after-noon. All the guests, including Irena and her family, would fly in on Saturday beforehand.

Nico still couldn't get over the fact that three weeks ago he'd gone to Irena's as a sin-gle man, and this afternoon he was bringing his former lover and beautiful daughter to his home. Things like this just didn't happen in normal life.

"Baba? Where are we exactly?"

He smiled. "We're on Sithonia, one of the three legs jutting into the Aegean from Salonica. I've been driving us along the coast of the Chalkidiki Peninsula." The road wound through the base of the green mountains, making a contrast to the turquoise waters of the Aegean. Nico always found it a breathtaking sight.

"It's so beautiful, but I thought I saw lightning above the mountains."

"We get it in summer, but it won't stop us from enjoying Sarti Beach tomorrow."

"Where's your villa?"

He could see Alexa through the rearview mirror. She was eyeing scenery she'd never viewed. By the look on her beautiful face, she was entranced.

"On the mountain overlooking the beach. You'll love the purity of the sand and water. It's not too deep."

Perfect for a mermaid with chestnut hair who loved to play in the water for hours. The vision of a young Alexa who'd enthralled him from day one flashed into his mind. They were occurring more often, disturbing him whether awake or asleep.

One more curve on the road and a view of Mount Athos opened up in the distance. The sight brought exclamations from everyone. "Ooh, I'd love to climb that with Kristos!" Dimitra exclaimed.

Nico chuckled. "I'm afraid you can't."

"Why not?"

"No women are allowed," her grandfather interjected. "It's forbidden."

"That's the most absurd thing I ever heard! What goes on there, Papoú?"

Nico's eyes met Alexa's through the mirror. Hers were smiling. Their daughter was a delight to both of them.

"You'd be surprised. It's the center of Eastern Orthodox monasticism. There are over twenty monasteries under the direct jurisdiction of the Ecumenical Patriarch of Constantinople. Not even female animals are allowed."

"Are you serious? That's incredible. I didn't realize. You always know everything."

"Not everything, but close."

Nico liked the older man very much. At Gavril's remark he burst into laughter along with Alexa, unable to remember the last time he'd enjoyed himself this much. Years in fact.

Being with Alexa had everything to do with this change in him. When he'd taken her to the vineyard recently, he'd meant what he'd said to her about forgetting the past. It *was* over. Inexplicably his anger seemed to have dissipated and his life had taken on a whole new meaning.

"We're almost home." He took a private road that wound up the mountainside to his white villa.

"You've got to be kidding me," Dimitra murmured after they arrived. "This is the most fabulous place I've ever seen in my life!" She undid her seat belt and turned to him. "I love it, Baba. I love you." In the next breath she threw her arms around him.

Nico's throat swelled with emotion as he kissed her cheek. "When I bought this place, I never imagined the day would come when my very own daughter would be here with me. I love you too," he said in a thick tone. "What do you say we get out so I can help your grandfather? He's had to sit for a long time."

"You're right. Since the moment I knew you were my father, my head's been spinning. I don't know what I'm doing and have only been thinking of my own happiness." Nico adored his daughter and felt the same way.

Just then they heard the whir of rotor blades. A helicopter was landing at the rear of the villa. "That'll be your fiancé."

She turned to get out. "I feel like I'm in a dream."

Nico could relate.

Within seconds Kristos came running. The two lovebirds threw their arms around each other. Nico glanced at Alexa who was getting out of her side of the car. He took her grand-father's wheelchair from the trunk.

"Here you go, Gavril. I'll have you com-fortable in a hurry." The older man deserved anything Nico could do for him after he'd sacrificed his life helping raise their daugh-ter all these years.

"I'm fine, Nico."

Thanos and Anna, the married couple who looked after his place and served in many capacities, came out to carry the luggage in-side.

Alexa stayed by her grandfather as Nico wheeled him through the sprawling, one-story villa to a guest room. Together they helped him get settled. "Anna will bring you a tray of food. Alexa's room is next door to you."

Gavril caught his arm. "You treat me like a king. Now you go on and help the others."

"I'll be right back and we'll eat together," Alexa assured him. After giving him a kiss, she followed Nico to the next guest room.

"Dimitra's room is at the end of the hall."

She walked to the window that overlooked the beach. "This spacious, airy villa is incredible, Nico. There's still a view since the light hasn't disappeared yet. You and your wife must have been beyond happy here."

The mention of Raisa jolted him because he hadn't been thinking about her at all. What was wrong with him? "We lived in a villa in Salonica. After she died, I sold it and bought this one."

Alexa looked over at him. "I'm sorry. I spoke without thinking."

"You have nothing to apologize for. Say whatever you want. When I'm in town and have to stay over, I use the apartment above the office. If you'd like to freshen up, I'll see to settling Dimitra and have food sent to you and Gavril."

Her eyes filled. "Thank you for being this wonderful to us."

"I can't do enough for our daughter." In truth he couldn't do enough for Alexa at this point. She'd handled the responsibility of raising their daughter alone, without him. He suffered over those missing years when he'd had no part in loving her and raising Dimitra from babyhood to the age she was now. The three of them had been cheated of that time together.

If he closed his eyes, nothing seemed to have changed. Her words and the way she said them made him believe they'd gone back in time to those three weeks when he'd lost his heart.

But there was a problem because when he opened them, his mermaid had grown into a stunning, sophisticated woman, a mother who had a career and responsibilities. Did she long for those days when they were so much in love, nothing else mattered?

Raisa had been very much aware of Nico's feelings for Mara. Now that she was gone, did he have the right to be thinking about Mara all over again? Did he deserve a second chance at happiness with her? Before this weekend was out, he wanted to take her out on the beach and spend time alone with her.

But did he dare? Would she want to be with him again like that?

Riddled with questions and guilt, he left the room.

The Saturday announcement party with family and a few close friends had put permanent smiles on the faces of the engaged couple. Most everyone had enjoyed the swimming pool. Alexa had preferred to walk around taking pictures with her phone, many of them of Nico.

All the fabulous catered food and music had made it an unforgettable day followed by professional picture taking to preserve memories. Though Nico's parents and sister couldn't have been nicer to Alexa and her grandfather, the two of them stayed close to Irena and her son Yanni.

Before all the guests had to leave, Alexa took Irena to her bedroom. It was there she shared the second letter Nico had sent her. As Irena read it, tears trickled down her cheeks.

"This gives me chills, Alexa."

"It did the same thing to me the first time I read it. I'd just been in your home with you the day before. Everything Nico wrote about Tio and you was true, down to your beautiful red hair."

She stared at Alexa. "It's unbelievable that my son met your daughter. What were the chances?"

"I know. He's the best!"

"So is she. I'm crazy about her. But I'm talking about Nico."

Alexa blinked. "What do you mean?"

"When he couldn't find you, he changed and was never the same again. I know because Tio and I helped him search for you. He was so in love and so heartbroken when he couldn't find you, it really wasted him for a long, long time. Now suddenly you've reappeared in his life, with *his* daughter no less. The change in him is more dramatic than you can imagine."

"But he got married!"

"Yes." Irena put a hand on her arm. "He realized he couldn't live on hope forever and she was a lovely person who adored him. But she knew you'd been the love of his life. If she'd lived and they'd had a baby to love, I have no doubts it would have helped him to be happier."

Alexa shook her head. "Her death was so terrible."

"Agreed, but he's handled it surprisingly well. What he's never gotten over is the loss of you. Not really. That's why I can tell you that your presence has brought about a miraculous healing. The sorrow he's worn like a burden since the first time I met him, is gone. Today he's a new man and that's all to do with you."

Irena's confession thrilled her. "Thank you for telling me this, but the fact remains, I did a terrible thing not to let him know I was pregnant at the very beginning. If I disgust you for what I held back, you're being very kind to me. It means more to me than you know."

"Alexa…if I'd been in your situation at that age, when Nico's parents were so prominent and your grandfather's career was at stake, I know I wouldn't have told Tio."

She wiped her eyes. "You're just saying that because you're such a good person."

"No. I'm telling you the truth. Tio's parents didn't approve of his relationship with me. I didn't come from a family of privilege. They did everything in their power to dissuade him from being with me. We eloped so they couldn't stop us, while he was still training in the military."

Alexa blinked in disbelief. "I didn't know that."

"It's taken a long time to win them over. I'm still not there yet in their eyes. Thank you for showing me this." Her voice caught. "It's another proof that Tio really did love me."

She started to give the letter back, but Alexa refused it. "Nico's letters provided me the same proof. You keep it and read it whenever you want. Now give me a minute to change into my bathing suit. It's a beautiful night and I feel like a swim before going to bed. You stay in here. When I'm ready, I'll walk you out to say goodbye."

Irena nodded, already reading the letter again.

Alexa left her to go in the bathroom to change. After putting on her beach robe she grabbed a big towel to take with her.

The two women hugged hard before they left the bedroom. Irena was quickly becoming a close friend. Alexa walked her out of the villa to the helicopter pad to see her off. Nico had gone to find Yanni. All the other guests had left.

While Dimitra and Kristos talked and ate on the patio with her grandfather, Alexa told them she was going to walk down the road to the beach. The sun hadn't set yet. It was a sight she wanted to see and told them she'd be back before long to help her grandfather get to bed.

Irena had given Alexa a lot to think about and she needed to be alone with her thoughts as she made her way toward the sea below. Nico couldn't have found a more enchanting spot on earth to live. She hoped she could be forgiven for being happy he hadn't lived here with his wife.

When she reached the beach, she slipped off her beach robe and put it on top of the towel before walking into the gentle sea. At any second the sun would drop below the horizon.

Getting in the water with Nico had been one of their greatest pleasures during those three weeks years ago. But to want to be alone with him now would be asking too much, even if she wanted to believe Irena. Alexa didn't doubt Nico was happy to finally know the truth about everything, but that didn't mean the sight of her made him want to go back to where they'd left off.

The other day in his office, he hadn't followed through and kissed her senseless the way he'd once done. He'd held back, which told Alexa she didn't dare imagine all had been forgiven.

For another thing, Nico couldn't have been celibate all this time since his wife's death.

There had to be a woman he was seeing right now. This weekend Nico had been the ultimate host, but once they were all back in Salonica tomorrow, he'd be free to see any woman he wanted. To imagine that Alexa could be an intimate part of his life again sounded almost beyond the realm of possibility.

How would he feel to know Alexa was longing to get back in his arms and stay there? While she'd been at his villa, she'd been able to handle being around him because other people had provided a buffer. Giannina, among others, had pulled her aside.

She'd said she'd like to go to lunch with her next week so they could talk. Apparently she'd forgiven Alexa enough for what she'd done to her brother to extend the olive branch. Alexa liked her and had agreed to meet her.

But now that everyone had gone, Alexa was prey to her emotions. Needing to rid herself of doubts and unassuaged longings, she swam hard until she'd worn herself out. As she swam toward the beach, she realized she wasn't alone.

CHAPTER SEVEN

"Nico—"

He looked like a Greek god as he walked into the water wearing his black trunks. "The family told me you were down here. I decided to join you."

Her heart was beating way too fast to be healthy. She started treading water. "I couldn't resist. Thanks to you, the party was a huge success, and this place is paradise."

Nico swam around her, reminding her of those magical nights in the sea years ago. "Our daughter just told me she's never been so happy in her life."

"I believe it."

His gaze pierced her. "What about you, Alexa? Are *you* happy?"

Being with Nico again had brought her an out-of-this-world kind of happiness. "You have no idea. Our daughter is finally getting to know her long-lost father, and she's engaged to be married to a very remarkable man I'm already crazy about." She smiled. "I'll ask you the same question."

He came closer. "You want to know if I'm happy?"

She had trouble swallowing. Her desire for him was so great, she thought she'd go crazy if he didn't reach for her. "Yes. Less than a month ago you had no idea what was going to happen and how it would affect your entire universe."

"That's the perfect way to describe it. When I kept getting those unopened letters and couldn't find you after I returned home, I knew my universe would never be the same again. Yet here you are tonight, bringing me more happiness than I deserve."

His answer thrilled her, but it puzzled her too. "What do you mean, deserve?"

"I'm not the person I once was."

His words haunted her. "I could say the

same thing about myself. Time changes all of us."

It hurt that the fun-loving man she worshipped had all of a sudden reverted to his more solemn self once more. Something troubling had to be going on inside him. She didn't know what to say and started swimming toward the beach. He followed her out of the water. Alexa reached for the towel to dry herself off.

Nico did the same thing. "If you've had enough, I'll drive you up to the villa."

"Thank you."

He didn't even want to walk in the sand with her for a few minutes? That was so unlike the Nico of the past. But what could she expect if he didn't love her the way he once had? Irena said he'd changed, but something prevented Nico from reaching for her physically.

She slipped on her beach robe and they made their way to the estate car parked where the private road ended. Her attraction to him had never been stronger, but she couldn't forget he'd found love with Raisa and had married her. Maybe her memory was holding him back. Nor could she deny the fact that she'd caused pain to the two people she loved most. To expect feelings or attraction from Nico at this point wasn't realistic.

It only took a minute to reach the villa. "Thank you so much for this fabulous party, Nico. Dimitra has been glowing. So has Kristos. Irena loves you for being so devoted to her and her family. Everything good has happened because of you."

She got out of the car without his help and hurried to the patio. Nico followed. "Come on, Grandpa. I don't know about you, but I'm exhausted," Alexa said.

"We appreciate all you've done, Nico," her grandfather assured him, then looked at Dimitra and Kristos. "You two need some time alone. I'm ready."

Dimitra got up. "Good night, Papoú, Mama. See you both in the morning. Thank you for everything." She kissed both of them and turned to her father. "Oh, Baba, this party has been so perfect. Thank you with all my heart."

Alexa watched father and daughter embrace and then pushed the wheelchair inside and through the house to her grandfather's bedroom. She helped him undress and get into bed.

"Looks like you and Dimitra are on a normal footing again."

She glanced at him. "We're getting there, with Nico's help." Alexa wished she could say the same about herself and Nico. "He has turned my nightmare into something we can all live with. He'll never know how grateful I am. Now I'm going to say good-night and see you in the morning. You've got your phone. If you need anything, call me and I'll come running. Good night."

Nico went to work the next week, but by the time the board of directors meeting ended on Friday, he realized he'd been worthless. He was no longer the same man who'd been running the Angelis empire. In the last four weeks his world had undergone an upheaval of biblical proportions.

After all these years he finally had answers to the questions that had tortured him. Alexa was alive and living in Salonica, not France. Dimitra was proving to be the most enchanting daughter any father could imagine having. To find out he'd had a child of his body with the woman he'd loved beyond all else had completely changed his vision of life.

By now the news had gone out through the media. Years ago the plane crash that had killed Nico's wife and unborn child had been sensationalized. Now came even more sensational news surrounding him. The recently appointed CEO of the Angelis Corporation had an eighteen-year-old daughter, but his deceased wife hadn't been the mother. Furthermore, the mother proved to be the granddaughter of the former Greek ambassador to Cyprus and Canada.

Kristos hadn't been spared either. His plan to marry the daughter of Nico Angelis in the near future had been spread all over the media. Sadly the horror of the car crash that had killed his father, a vice president in the Papadakis Shipping Lines, had also been brought to the surface once more.

Nico had known it would all come out.

Much as he wished the news hadn't hurt their families, he'd been too overjoyed with his daughter to let it affect him. But he worried for Alexa and the impact it had made on her. By the time the board meeting had ended late Friday afternoon, his concern drove him to phone her. He was glad for the excuse.

All week he'd resisted the temptation to call her. After Nico had driven them back to Salonica on Sunday and helped her grandfather inside, he'd been forced to face the truth. He hadn't wanted to leave her. If it had been possible, he would have asked her to stay at the villa for a week or longer.

That moment in the water with Alexa had changed him. When the family had told him she'd gone down for a swim, he couldn't join her fast enough, and there she was. He kept looking at her gorgeous face and hair. It was then he realized he wasn't angry. Not anymore. He found himself wanting to be with her again in every sense of the word. He wanted her in his arms and his bed.

Being around Alexa for the weekend hadn't been nearly long enough. To have to say goodbye Sunday afternoon had been difficult, yet she'd shown no regret that he was leaving. He couldn't stand the separation any longer.

With determination he reached for his cell and made the call. She answered on the third ring.

"Nico?" She sounded surprised. Her reaction deflated him. What had he expected? That she would sound breathless the way she once did waiting to hear from him?

There was a lot he wanted to discuss with her, but not over the phone. "I'll make this quick. Do you have plans for this evening?"

"Only to watch a soccer match with my grandfather. We're eating dinner right now."

That ruled out his first suggestion. "Would you mind if I came by to pick you up? We could go for a ride. It won't take long. I need your advice about Dimitra."

"Is everything all right?" Alarm had tinged her voice. "I know you've been with her several times this week."

"We're fine, but I'm a new father and would like your input."

"I'm not sure how much help I can be. How soon do you want to come?"

"Shall we say half an hour, or do you need more time?"

"No, no. I'll be ready. See you soon."

He hung up, relieved she hadn't turned him down. Once he'd showered and changed out of his suit, he took off for the Filo home. She met him at the door bringing a faint floral fragrance with her that was new. In those pleated white pants and fitted khaki-colored top, Nico had a hard time not staring at the feminine mold of her body.

After he helped her in the car, he drove them down to the beach and parked near the water.

"We've been here before," she murmured.

He shut off the engine and turned to her, studying her stunning profile. The sun would be going down soon and the golden-hour light brought out the gold highlights of her hair. How many times had he kissed her and played with it, never wanting to stop. "The beach was our home. It seems natural to come here. Let's walk."

Alexa removed her shoes and got out. After stepping on the sand she looked at him with a hint of anxiety. "What did you want to ask me about Dimitra?"

Damn. She was feeling uncomfortable with him. They'd never had that trouble in their past life together. "I'll get to that in a minute. First, I've been worried about the coverage in the news the other night. How are you and Gavril handling it?"

"We're fine. He's no longer working for the government, and I won't be working at the university until the end of August. Neither of us is in the limelight."

"What about Dimitra?"

"If it bothered her, she hasn't said. I know

it's because she's so involved with Kristos. None of us has to face people the way *you* do on a daily basis. Before long the news will die down for us. Let's hope for you too since you didn't ask for any of this." The tremor in her voice tugged on his emotions.

"Don't worry about me."

She finally turned to him. "How can you say that? This whole situation hasn't been fair to you or your family." Her eyes, like precious green gems, filmed over. "If I'd done the right thing the moment I knew I was pregnant, this would nev—"

"Stop," he broke in on her. "We promised not to go there again. You did what you felt had to be done at the time. It's over. I realized that while we were at the villa last weekend and I saw you in the water. It reminded me of our past. Not only were you young, you weren't my wife when we made love. I fought it until that last night. The blame falls on me."

She made a strange sound. "Don't forget I was the most willing participant on earth,

Nico. I had no shame. You were my whole life."

And mine. "Love hit us hard, but make no mistake. I'm the reason for your pregnancy and take full responsibility, even if it is nineteen years too late. I should have known better than to act on my desires before our marriage could take place." He'd been out of control. "I should have been there when you had our baby. Tell me what it was like."

"I was terrified!" Then a smile lit her face. "The pains started early on a Thursday morning and were unreal. After they'd grown five minutes apart, my grandmother drove me to the hospital. Dimitra was born at eight thirty-two in the evening. My grandfather came to the hospital two hours before the delivery."

Nico groaned. He reached for her hand as they walked. "You were in labor twelve hours?"

She nodded. "The doctor told me that was pretty normal. I could hear Dimitra cry while she was being delivered. It was like a gurgle at first. They put her across my chest and I'll never forget that feeling of holding her for the first time. She was beautiful, with olive skin and dark hair like yours. I wanted you there more than anything."

Nico could hardly breathe thinking about it. "How much did she weigh?"

"Seven pounds, two ounces and she was twenty inches long. Perfect. I stayed in the hospital two days so I could learn how to nurse her. She took to it fast. I have so many pictures and home movies. Dimitra will show all of them to you. The grandparents doted on her as much as I did."

"I can't wait to see everything." Hearing about the delivery made Nico hunger for every detail of her life from the time they'd been apart.

"What did you want to talk to me about?"

He stopped walking and let go of her hand. "I wondered what you would think about a weekend cruise on the yacht, just you, Dimitra, Gavril and me. We could leave on a Friday afternoon and come back Sunday. I thought we could visit the island of Samos."

Her eyes widened in surprise. "You used to tell me how much you loved going there with your friends."

Nico had the satisfaction of knowing she hadn't forgotten all the things they'd talked about. "Dimitra will love it too. At night you could get out all those pictures and home movies to entertain us. I only have one question. Do you think our daughter could stand to be away from Kristos for two nights?"

She darted him one of those impish smiles he remembered, almost giving him a heart attack. "I'm the wrong person to ask. During those three weeks years ago, I resented every second we weren't together. But Dimitra's case is different. She'll have the incentive of spending hours with her newly discovered *baba*. I can't imagine anything being more wonderful for her. You wouldn't need me with you."

He'd been afraid she'd say that, and he refused to let the fact that he hadn't loved Raisa as he should have get in the way now. He wanted to be with Alexa and needed to convince her. "You're wrong. This is still new to both of us and I want her to be comfortable. That can only happen if you and Gavril are there too. One of the stewards will be happy to help him with whatever he might need so please don't worry. If you're in agreement, would you broach the subject with her and let me know how she feels? I can arrange for any weekend."

"Spoken like the CEO who makes the rules," she teased.

"My only perk."

"Be honest. The best one." Talking with her like this made the lost years fade for a little while.

A smile lifted at the corner of her luscious mouth. "Do you know while we were together, I never realized what kind of life was waiting for you in your father's company. I'm embarrassed to think I didn't have a clue what responsibilities you would inherit one day."

Nico chuckled. "My problem was, I *did* know what was waiting for me, and it got in the way of my wanting to spend every second of my life with you."

She blushed. "I'm afraid I was oblivious to everything except just being with you. Monika's mother teased me mercilessly about being good for nothing while I waited for you to get off work. I helped clean and cook when Monika and I didn't go out, but my mind was constantly on you. Dimitra is just as bad when she's waiting for Kristos to come."

Her smile swept him away. "Do you think she'd like to be with the two of us for a few days?"

"I'll talk to her, Nico, and let you know."

"Do you think she might be home now?"

"I'm not sure. Let's find out and go back. My grandfather will be happy if I can watch the last of the match with him."

After Nico saw her to the door, Alexa watched him drive off. Once again, he took her heart with him. Nothing had changed. She would always hunger for him, but that hunger could never be assuaged if he didn't want her just as badly.

I should have been there when you had our baby. Those words Nico had said earlier reminded her how she'd kept him and their daughter apart. But as he'd said, it was over and there was no point in dwelling on it.

She closed the door and walked through to the study. If Dimitra showed excitement over the idea of an outing on the yacht with her parents, Alexa would go as a favor to Nico. But that would have to be the end of family trips. After all, the three of them weren't a family in the proverbial sense.

When broached the next morning, Dimitra acted overjoyed at the prospect. She phoned her father immediately. Alexa heard laughter from their daughter who said, "I can live without Kristos that long, Baba." The rapport between the two of them thrilled Alexa. Dimitra had been missing this all her life, but no longer.

By now it was July and the weather had grown hotter. The following Friday Nico came by for them and loaded his car with their bags. Before long they boarded the yacht and were shown to their staterooms. Even though Dimitra had already been on the yacht to meet his family, she walked around in a dazed condition. And she wasn't the only one—the opulence exceeded Alexa's expectations. Again she marveled that this had been Nico's life, but at seventeen she hadn't understood.

But Monika had known. Only too well.

Alexa needed to put all that away. In the car last week Nico had told her to stop ruminating. The past was over. So be it!

Friday night the four of them ate dinner and watched the home movies. Tears washed Gavril's face to see his beloved Iris holding the new baby. Before long Alexa and her daughter were also in tears. Nico watched the scenes at the hospital. At one point he turned to her. His dark eyes shone. "How incredible all this was filmed."

"Thank my grandfather. He insisted."

Gavril smiled. "There's much more to see."

They stayed up late watching movies of their home in Ottawa, Dimitra's different birthday parties. There were even films showing Alexa's parents when she'd been a little girl, and Gavril's investiture as ambassador in Ottawa, which Iris had taken.

No one wanted to stop, but Alexa eventually called a halt. Not only because her grandfather was tired and needed to go to bed, but because her heart couldn't handle any more memories that didn't include Nico. He'd missed out on his daughter's entire life until now.

By morning, the yacht had reached Samos in the Eastern Aegean. Nico told them it was the birthplace of the famous mathematician Pythagoras. Gavril insisted on staying next to the yacht swimming pool to read while the three of them went ashore. A small motorboat dropped them off and left them to explore the mountainous island.

They were a real family. All three of them wore shorts and T-shirts. Nico took them to his favorite places to see waterfalls, fields of wildflowers, a church on a summit and fantastic views. After a long hike, they reached the main village. Dimitra wanted to stop at an embroidery shop to buy a small gift for Irena and Nico's mother.

"While you do that, your mother and I will walk to that alfresco café jutting out in the water and order us an early dinner."

"I might be a while since I promised to phone Kristos."

Nico's smile took Alexa back nineteen years. "Understood." Dimitra took off, eager to talk to her beloved.

To Alexa's surprise, Nico took her arm as they walked along the beachfront. The action had been so natural, she realized he'd forgotten for a moment that they weren't a couple. But she'd forgotten nothing. His touch shot darts of desire through her body. The sensation caused her breath to catch. She wondered if he had any idea what the contact was doing to her.

Nico said, "Is there any doubt our daughter is wildly in love?"

"None at all. Did you notice she ambles over rocks and boulders exactly the way you do, Nico? Like father, like daughter."

When he chuckled, it reminded her of what Irena had told her at the engagement party about Nico. *I can tell you that your presence has brought about a miraculous healing.* Alexa wouldn't have known what he was like before he'd learned he had a daughter, but today even his eyes wore a smile.

He was so striking, every woman in sight, young or old, stared at him. What special female had caught his attention these days? Alexa shouldn't care or even want to know. But the possibility that he spent some of his nights with another woman who had to be crazy about him was consuming her.

They found a table overlooking the water and a waiter came right over. Nico eyed her. "The sautéed shrimp here is a specialty of the house. Would you like to try it?"

"I'd love it."

"I promise you will."

He ordered them wine. She felt like they'd

gone back to the past. *But you're in the present now, Alexa. Remember that.* "How are your friends adjusting to the fact that you have a daughter who now claims some of your time?"

"Tio's gone, and I've never socialized much with my business associates. As for women, there's been no one recently." That particular piece of news shouldn't have pleased her. "Any rare free time has been spent with family and Irena. I enjoy scuba diving with Yanni and Kristos."

Alexa sipped her wine. "I never did learn."

"You're welcome to join us if you ever want to try it. If you remember, I promised to teach you one day."

As if she could forget anything he'd said or done. "Thank you, Nico. Maybe I'll take you up on it."

"When?"

She laughed out loud. "That sounds just like you. I'd say whenever we both have time."

"I'll make time."

"So will I. These days I'm working on a

project that will keep me busy for another couple of months." Alexa wanted to do anything with him, but didn't want to sound too eager. All she could do was wait for more signs.

"That sounds intriguing," he murmured. "Tell me about it."

Their food came and they started to eat.

"After I got my BEd to teach, I went on to obtain a master's degree in classical mythology. Later on I compiled a series of myths I could water down for grade-school children. It took several years to find an agent. In time a publisher got interested. I worked with their art staff and eventually my collection came out in both English and Greek."

He stared as if he'd never seen her before. "Congratulations." His deep voice curled through her. "I remember how much you loved them."

"They fascinated me. The collection had enough success that I was encouraged to compile another series of myths for young adults."

"You amaze me you could do it at all."

"I believe the experience has been cathartic for me. I've worked on this collection with a different concept in mind by exploring a basic emotion and making it the title of each story."

"I'm impressed by your brilliance."

She smiled. "I didn't write those myths, Nico. All I've done is try to present them in an interesting way for teenagers."

His eyes narrowed. "Have you included Hera's myth?"

"No. I—I couldn't." Her voice faltered.

"I'm glad. That myth needs to be buried forever."

Oh, Nico...

Alexa took a deep breath. "If you want to read something creative and historic right out of my grandfather's incredible mind, you should sink your teeth into his first drafts of his ambassador memoirs on Cyprus. Then he'll start on his book about his experiences in Canada."

Nico finished the last of his wine. "I hope

you mean that and make them available to me. More and more I'm realizing what an exceptional man Gavril is. He's had the job of being husband, father, grandfather, then starting again being a father to you and to Dimitra, all the while handling the difficult job of two ambassadorships. Since you've inherited his genes, it's no wonder you're a star in your own right."

Heat filled her cheeks. "Hardly that."

"Do you write under your own name?"

"I've always gone by Alexa Soriano Remis. Soriano was my grandmother's maiden name."

"I noticed that on the birth certificate. Maybe we'll find a copy of one of your books in the bookstore here on the island."

She smiled. "No, but there are copies in the Aristotle University library in Salonica."

"How soon will your new collection be published?"

"I should have it finished by the end of this summer. Before the fall semester starts at the university, I plan to fly to Ottawa and work for a few days with the artists again. Then we'll see."

Nico ate the last two delicious shrimps she'd left on the platter. "Speaking of that timetable, Kristos called me at work yesterday. He and Dimitra want to get married before the end of the summer."

"I know, but that's only seven weeks from now."

He nodded. "Irena still wants them to wait a year."

"Oh, dear." She half moaned the words. "Another battle."

"Has Dimitra mentioned it to you?"

"Yes. Now that they're engaged, they don't want to wait and at this point I understand. Frankly I don't want to fight with her, not after this upheaval in our lives. I'm afraid to do anything to ruin the bit of peace I've achieved with her."

"I'll tell Irena what you said."

"How do you feel about it, Nico?" She looked into his dark eyes, worrying about him. "You've just discovered you have a daughter. Now she wants to get married. There's so little time for the two of you to enjoy each other."

He sat back in the chair. "I'm so overjoyed to have a daughter, I'm planning to take each day as it comes to the very end of my life. I hope you'll allow me to pay for their wedding whenever it occurs. I'm her father and it's time I did my part."

They'd been so engrossed in their conversation, Alexa hadn't noticed their daughter who'd approached carrying a bag of things she'd bought. Dimitra stood staring at the two of them with an expectant look on her face.

CHAPTER EIGHT

"I HEARD YOU talking about my wedding, Mama. Is it all right with you if Kristos and I get married at the end of the summer term at the university? It'll be the perfect time before classes start again. We've been talking about it on the phone."

"Honey, I'm fine with the idea, but you need to discuss it with his mother. She'd rather you waited a year."

"But we don't want to wait that long." Dimitra sat in a chair. "You talk to her, Baba. Kristos says she listens to you about everything."

Alexa exchanged a private glance with Nico before she said, "Do you know why she's asking you to wait?"

"Kristos just told me. His grandfather wants us to put off marriage until he turns twenty-five and knows what he's doing. That's why he didn't come to our engagement party."

"I see."

"His mother is worried he'll hold Kristos back in the company if he doesn't conform. But Kristos says he'll resign if necessary and find another job in order to marry me now."

Alexa and Nico exchanged a glance. Suddenly her conversation with Irena in the bedroom about her elopement with Tio made perfect sense.

Nico covered his daughter's hand. "I'll talk to Irena and assure her that if Kristos needs another job, he can come to me."

"You mean it?" She jumped up and threw her arms around him. "I have to call him right now and tell him."

"Don't you want to eat first?"

"I couldn't. Excuse me. I'll be back in a minute."

The second she'd gone, Alexa looked at Nico. "Was Tio's father as controlling of him as he is of Kristos?"

His brows furrowed. "Worse. He's the antithesis of my father. If Irena hadn't been waiting for Tio when he returned from military service, he would have left Greece to find his own way."

"She told me they eloped. Nico, if you end up helping Kristos, won't you be making an enemy?"

His features tautened. "We became enemies the moment he found out I was Tio's best man at their secret wedding and helped them pay for their first apartment."

"You did that?" Nico had always been more generous than anyone she'd ever known. That quality in him had never changed, making her love him all the more.

He nodded. "His father cut off all his funds, but in time he had to make peace with Tio because Tio's mother threatened to divorce him if he didn't. It would have caused a scandal. The mansion Irena lives in now came from Kristos's grandmother on Irena's side."

"I can't believe he would threaten his son like that."

"It got ugly, but the good news is, Tio married Irena. They took vows at that church we visited earlier today on our hike."

A gasp escaped her lips. "What a beautiful place for a wedding! Why didn't you tell Dimitra while we were up there? It would have meant everything to her."

"That's Irena's story to tell. She walks a thin line when it comes to Tio's father. He wants to turn his grandson into the personification of himself, but it'll never happen."

"That's terribly sad, but how blessed she and her boys are to be able to turn to you. And Dimitra now too."

With her emotions spilling all over the place, she got up from the table and left the restaurant to catch up with her daughter, who was standing beneath a tree near the entrance.

Dimitra hung up, then hurried toward Alexa. "It's settled. Kristos is home and he's going to talk to his mother right now. Baba has made everything perfect. I'm so happy I can hardly stand it! I love him so much."

So do I, honey. So do I.

Nico walked over to them. "Do you want to do a little more shopping before we go?"

"Maybe another time, but I'd rather go back to the yacht. Kristos will be calling me soon. We have a lot to talk over."

The amused look in Nico's eyes told Alexa nothing was more important than that. She knew he was remembering how it was between the two of them years ago. To be together was all that had mattered. It lightened Alex's heart that Nico acted so happy about it. She wanted to protect him from any more hurt.

They followed Dimitra to the pier. He helped them climb in the motorboat that drove them out to the yacht.

She turned to him. "How come you never took us on board your family yacht years ago?" she whispered.

He studied her features. "I wanted you to myself with no staff around. Do you wish I had?"

"What do you think?"

Something flickered in his eyes. "I'll tell you later when we're alone."

Alexa hoped he meant it. Their arms brushed against each other, igniting her senses. He could probably tell how she trembled at his touch. If he only knew what was going on inside her.

Once aboard, Dimitra and Alexa went to their staterooms. The steward told her that her grandfather was in the club lounge enjoying his dinner while he watched TV. Alexa would join him in a little while, but right now she was hot and sticky. After changing into her swimming suit, she hurried to the pool and dove in the deep end. A good swim could help dampen the desire Nico had aroused in her.

Nico headed straight for the pool and was doing laps when he saw Alexa coming. His heart leaped and he swam underwater toward her. In her blue bikini, no woman would ever look as good to him as she did. He reached for her hips and turned her over before they broke water.

"Nico—" she gasped. Her hands clutched his shoulders.

"Kind of like old times isn't it." Unable to stop what was happening, he cupped her face and hungrily kissed the luscious mouth he'd been longing for. He'd never been able to get enough.

To his joy he was met with an equally hungry response from her. They clung to each other as if their lives depended on it, shaking him to the very core. He felt they'd gone back in time. The action took them under the water. He continued kissing her as he pulled her over to the side.

"You shouldn't have done that," she cried once they'd had a chance to catch their breath. After what had just transpired, he didn't think he'd get his back. How many years had he dreamed of being with her again like this? By now she was holding on to the side of the pool with both hands, refusing to look at him.

"It came naturally for both of us, so don't deny it."

"I'm not," she answered with honesty, but turned away.

Nico wasn't ready to let her go and held her so her back lay against his chest. Her whole beautiful body trembled. He moved her hair to kiss the side of her neck. "Don't you think it's time we talked about us?"

"I guess I'm a little afraid."

"Of what?" He refused to be put off by her despairing tone. "The fact that you're in my arms?"

"I didn't know you were in the pool. I suppose this was inevitable, but we're not the same people and can't pick up where we left off."

"Agreed, but we're still on fire for each other. So why don't we talk about our future."

"Be serious," she begged him.

Nico wrapped his arm around her waist, determined to make her listen. "I'm deadly serious."

"What are you saying?"

He held her tighter. "My wife and unborn baby died, depriving me of the chance of becoming a father. Monika Gataki prevented me from raising our baby. You have no idea what it did to me to watch those videos of you in the hospital with Dimitra that I was no part of."

Tears filled her eyes. "I'm so sorry, Nico. I was afraid you might be hurt by watching them, and I was right."

He nestled her closer. "What it did was make me want to have another baby with you."

She trembled. "That's impossible, Nico."

"Of course it isn't. You're free. So am I. We're both still young enough to have another baby and raise it together. There's no Monika to interfere this time."

"That's true, but—"

"But nothing," he broke in on her. "That's past history. I want a baby and you're the only woman on earth who can give me what I want."

Alexa whirled around still locked in his

arms. "There are other women out there who'd give anything to be your wife."

"But they can't give me another child as perfect as Dimitra. Only you can make that happen again. She needs a sibling. Don't you understand? I want to do what we'd planned long ago and get married, raise a family.

"Nothing has changed the chemistry between us. It's there, stronger than ever and you know it. We've missed the first nineteen years and aren't getting any younger. There's nothing to prevent our marriage now."

"Except that I killed something inside of you, Nico. I saw it in your eyes when I told you Dimitra was our daughter. Deny it all you want, but that pure love you felt for me before you left to go in the military isn't there anymore. It'll never come back."

"You don't know all that's going on inside of me."

"I know this much. I don't want anything to damage your relationship with Dimitra. Now that she's found you, she adores you. To ruin that would be the greatest tragedy of all."

He frowned. "What do you mean ruin?"

"Don't you see? If I started spending time with you, Dimitra would have to compete for your attention. She'd learn to resent me. I kept her to myself for eighteen years. But all that has changed now that she's found you." She broke into tears. "I refuse to stand in the way of the happiness you two bring to each other. I could never do that to either of you."

Alexa broke free of his arms and climbed out of the pool. Nico had no choice but to let her go for the moment. He did another ten laps to think about what she'd said. Her guilt was much worse than he'd imagined. Nico had his work cut out to free her of it.

A few minutes later Dimitra came out to the pool in her swimming suit, filled with excitement. Nico didn't imagine he'd ever get used to the joy of having a daughter, let alone one as satisfying in every way as Dimitra. She dropped a towel on a chair and dove in. When she emerged she said, "I'll never be able to thank you enough, Baba."

"What are you talking about?"

"You offered to help Kristos with a job if worse came to worse. Irena thought it over and has given him her blessing for our marriage to take place. We've tentatively settled on Saturday, the twenty-sixth of August. Mama says that date is fine for her. Will that work for you? I know how busy you are."

"Not too busy for anything as important as your wedding." Relief swept through Nico that Irena had capitulated. It fit in with a plan that had been forming in his mind. "That gives you seven weeks to arrange everything."

"After Papoú is in bed, let's find Mama and start planning. We might as well do it now while you're not at the office."

Contrary to what Alexa imagined in her mind, Dimitra showed no resentment of her mother and wanted both parents involved all the way. Nothing could have suited Nico better. The sooner Dimitra's wedding happened, the sooner Alexa wouldn't have an excuse.

"This is an opportune moment considering

you need to put your intent to marry declaration in the newspaper before anything else."

"That's what Kristos said."

"Your aunt Giannina will take care of it once it's written."

"I'm so lucky."

"That works both ways."

Nico would do his part as father of the bride-to-be without making Alexa uncomfortable. Following through with plans for the big event would provide legitimate opportunities for him to be with her. She wouldn't be able to fight their need for each other indefinitely.

"How about a race before we go in, Baba?"

"You're on!"

Racing his daughter back and forth proved to be the stuff dreams were made of. He'd never had so much fun. A little while later Alexa came out to find them, saving them from having to find her, dressed in white shorts and a white top. She sat on one of the chairs. "I decided to find out if you two were still alive."

"Baba swims like a fish, Mama. No one could ever beat him."

Alexa chuckled. "I found that out years ago. It's how we met."

"Tell me."

The blood rushed into her cheeks. "Well, he was racing his friends off his cruiser and we bumped into each other, causing him to lose. It was probably the one and only time he went down in defeat."

Nico's gaze fused with hers. "That's because I met up with a mermaid whose superpowers rendered me helpless."

It pleased him when she averted her eyes. He knew bringing up that memory had slipped past her defenses.

Dimitra climbed out of the pool. She dried off before sitting by her mother. "Did Mama really look like a mermaid?"

Nico swam over to the side near them. "Her hair was long back then, and she knew moves in the water that blew me away. All that was missing was her tail."

Dimitra laughed. "Great-grandma Iris was

a champion swimmer. She taught Mama from the time she was little. I can't wait to tell Kristos you thought Mama looked like a mermaid. Oh, just so you know, he's meeting us at the dock tomorrow at noon. We're going to see the priest at Saint Catherine's in Ano Poli. He wants to be married where their family has always worshipped."

"That's only natural," Alexa interjected. "It'll make Irena very happy."

Nico nodded. "I think it's the perfect choice, Dimitra. If Kristos's father were alive, he'd want it there too." He couldn't be more pleased that his own daughter would be married there. Tio would have exchanged vows with Irena in that centuries-old Byzantine church if circumstances had been different for them.

"I'm so glad you both agree. Now we're trying to decide on a place for the reception. Do you have any ideas, Baba? Mama and I have been talking about it, but we think you're the one who would know the best spot."

Nico had already given it thought. "I'd pick

the Macedonian Palace. Depending on the weather, you can hold the reception indoors or outside. The hotel is centrally located and easy to find for those coming from out of town."

"Kristos mentioned it, but it's expensive and—"

"But nothing," Nico broke in. "If that's his choice too, then we'll book it if that's all right with you, Alexa."

"I want what all of you want."

Good. "Then that will be one of my gifts to the bride. The other will be your wedding dress. I want you and your mother to shop your heads off for all the things you'll need."

"That's far too generous of you, Baba." Her eyes had teared up.

"You're my only child. A parent lives for a moment like this. Wouldn't you say, Alexa?"

"You know I would," she murmured in an emotional tone before getting up. "It looks like we've gotten the most important issues decided. Now if you'll excuse me, I need to check on your *papoú*, so I'll say good-night."

Dimitra jumped up. "I'll come with you. I promised I'd phone Kristos after we'd had this talk. Good night, Baba. I love you so much."

"Kalinikta, I kóri mou polytima."

Good night, my precious daughter.

The love in Nico's voice caused Alexa's eyes to close tightly for a moment. Nico would never know what those words had to mean to Dimitra, let alone to Alexa herself. He really did love his daughter! From the moment he'd known about her, he'd devoted himself to her. With the amount of time he gave her, you'd never know he was the famous Angelis CEO with huge responsibilities.

Dimitra lapped up that love like any child starving for a father's affection. There was a new glow about her that came from enjoying the security he gave her. Nico did something no one else could do.

Alexa realized he would have been just as attentive to Dimitra whether Alexa had contacted him the moment she'd known she was pregnant, or after she'd told him about Monika's revelation. It was too late to wish she hadn't kept them apart, but one thing she did know. Life was going to be wonderful from here on out for her daughter.

As for Nico, there was no doubt in her mind that whatever his circumstances—even marriage to another woman—he would have moved heaven and earth to have a relationship with Dimitra. Nico was a prince among men.

"Mama? Do you mind if I ask you something personal?" She'd come into Alexa's stateroom.

"Of course not. What is it?"

"Do you wish you could be with my father again? You know what I mean."

Alexa couldn't believe her daughter had asked her that question now, just after Alexa and Nico had shared that shattering kiss in the pool. "Oh, honey. That's all over with."

"I don't know. I've been watching the two of you and get the feeling you're both in a private world of your own half the time."

She bit her lip, pricked with guilt. "Has it worried you, because—"

"Worried me?" she cut in on her mother, sounding bewildered. "That's an odd thing to say. You should have been together and married as soon he'd returned from the military. That insane Monika wanted Baba for herself and did a monstrous thing to you."

"But that's old history, honey."

"You're right. Now that I know all the facts, how could I blame you for what you did? Your circumstances were horrendous at the time. Papoú agrees with me. So does Kristos's mother. She said she would have hidden the truth too if she'd been pregnant and had thought Kristos's father had only been having fun with her. But remember this: Monika hasn't won yet."

Those words staggered Alexa while Dimitra kept on talking.

"I hope you'll get back together with my father. Kristos wants the same thing for the two of you. Those other men who asked you to marry them were never good enough for you. And you couldn't have been interested in the man you went out with!"

"I'm not, honey. I said goodbye."

"Thank goodness. There's only one Baba. It's no wonder no other man ever came close." The words continued to pour out of her daughter's romantic soul. "You were right about him at seventeen. No other man is like him and never could be. Promise me you'll think about getting back with him."

Probably nothing could have shocked Alexa more. Not only had Dimitra forgiven her, she wanted her parents to get back together. It shook her to the foundations, leaving her speechless.

"I feel the same way about Kristos. He's my one and only. Good night, Mama." She gave her a hug and left the stateroom.

Besides Alexa's grandfather, Irena had a lot to do with Dimitra's ability to understand and forgive something so earth-shattering for her at the time. Alexa would have to find a way to thank her for what she'd done to help heal a wound she'd thought couldn't be healed.

She shivered after getting in bed, remembering what Nico had told her in the pool earlier. This evening he'd asked her to marry him. Dimitra's instincts hadn't been wrong about noticing the undercurrents between Alexa and Nico. But Alexa couldn't forget that this proposal had been prompted by a far different reason than the first one.

Nineteen-year-old Nico had been madly in love when they'd planned their marriage. Now everything was different. Since that time, Nico had lost his wife and unborn child. Furthermore, he'd be losing his newly found daughter to Kristos.

Tears poured from Alexa's eyes. She understood that nothing could ever take the place of Nico raising his own child from birth. Alexa had deprived him of that experience. If she did agree to marry him to give him another child to love, maybe that could help make up for what had happened.

But even if the unimaginable happened and they did marry, there'd be no guarantee she'd get pregnant again. Worse, Alexa could never expect the kind of love he'd once showered on her. She doubted they could get back the pure magic they'd shared.

She could imagine the question her grandfather would ask her. *Can you survive in a marriage where you don't believe Nico will ever feel for you what he once did? Be careful before you say yes.*

Alexa wrestled with that question throughout the night, but never found an answer. Early the next morning she got up and put on her bikini. Her grandfather would sleep another hour. That would give her time to work off emotions in the pool before everyone awakened.

A gorgeous day, already getting hot, greeted her as she hurried along the deck carrying her beach towel. Her heart slammed into her ribs when she saw Nico already in the pool.

He must have seen her coming and lounged against the side at the deep end, his arms outstretched in a relaxed position. *Like a young Zeus who'd beguiled Io.*

"I'm glad to see you couldn't sleep either, and hoped you'd come out here early." His deep voice stirred her senses. "We'll be docking at noon and won't have a lot of time to talk alone."

Alexa sank down in one of the lounge chairs, knowing that if she dove in, he'd reach for her and there'd be no more talk. "I thought we discussed the important things about the upcoming wedding last night."

"Which one?"

Her heart thudded. "Nico—"

He swam to the side of the pool nearest her. "I've been thinking about it since you went to bed last night. When I first saw you at Irena's, I was incredulous that you'd had a baby with another man. But nothing has blotted out the image I've carried in my mind of the two of us all these years. That image intensified when you told me Dimitra was my daughter."

"I was so unfair to you." Her voice trembled.

"Then make it fair and marry me next Friday."

"What?"

He climbed out of the pool and walked over to her, dripping wet, and gave her a long, passionate kiss. "I told you last night I want another baby with you, and the idea hasn't left me alone. Maybe a son this time. Who knows how long it will take for you to get pregnant? We may not be as lucky as we were that night on my cruiser and can't afford to waste any more time."

She shook her head. "You're not making sense, and certainly not with our daughter's wedding coming up."

"You're wrong. We'll fly to Sarti Friday morning while Dimitra is at school, and marry in the Church of the Assumption. The priest and I are good friends."

Her heart was running away with her. "But we can't do it that fast, not with all the regulations."

"We can because I have sources in high places who'll waive the rules for us."

"You're serious!"

"How can you doubt it? Except for telling

Gavril our plans, our secret wedding will be private to the world. Afterward we'll spend several hours at the villa before we fly back to Salonica that evening without anyone being the wiser.

"Until Dimitra and Kristos are married, we'll slip away each evening before you have to get home to help your grandfather to bed. Once they're back from their honeymoon, we'll announce our marriage to the whole family. By then we might even be pregnant."

She got to her feet on unsteady legs. "Please don't say anything else. Y-You're not thinking clearly," she stammered, too alarmed, excited and terrified all at once to think.

"I've had five weeks to get my thoughts straight. Last night they became as crystal clear as the water on my private stretch of beach."

An almost primitive gleam entered his dark eyes. She knew what was going to happen before he swept her in his arms and they landed in the deep end of the pool. "I want another kiss from my mermaid who took a long swim away from me to the other side of the world. But she's back, and I'll make sure she never gets away from me again."

His mouth closed over hers, kissing her with a possessive intensity that overwhelmed her. Alexa could no more deny what she clamored for than she could stop breathing. It took her back to that time of pure rapture. But he hadn't said he loved her. Maybe she'd never hear those words.

Yet after losing his unborn baby, he wanted a baby so badly he'd asked her to marry him as soon as next Friday. Deep down she had to admit she would love another baby with him. He'd be the greatest father on earth. But nothing was that simple. Even though Dimitra had forgiven her enough to want her parents to get together, there were other obstacles Alexa couldn't imagine overcoming.

"Let me go, Nico," she begged, struggling to separate herself from him. "I can hear voices."

"I'll let you swim away as long as you promise to fly to Sarti with me on Friday.

Otherwise I'll tell Dimitra and your grand-father our plans right now while we're still on the yacht. The decision is yours."

"Nico, you can't!"

"They're coming."

She was desperate. "I'll think about it."

"You've got to do better than that." He had a ruthless side she'd never seen before. After what she'd done to him, it shouldn't surprise her.

"I promise." But it didn't mean she would marry him.

CHAPTER NINE

THE NEXT WEEK passed slowly for Nico and it wasn't until Thursday night that he finally went over to see Irena and told her his plans.

"I've never revealed something to you, but now I feel I must. When I married Raisa, I didn't love her the way I'd loved Alexa. I—"

"Say no more," Irena interrupted him with a smile. "I knew that Alexa had broken your heart, and I cheered the fact that you chose to get on with your life and marry Raisa. She knew it too, but she loved you so much, she married you anyway, knowing how you felt. She wanted any love you could give her, and I happen to know you made her very happy. She told me everything."

Nico shook her head. "I had no idea."

"I know, and I promised I'd never tell you. But now I can. So marry your Alexa knowing Raisa wanted you or no one else and the years you gave her were the happiest ones of her life. Now it's time to make Alexa happy again. She never married because you filled her heart so completely. That should tell you everything. I couldn't be happier for both of you."

Nico hugged her for a long time.

At nine o'clock Friday morning, he drove over to Alexa's on a burst of adrenaline. His daughter would already have left for class at the university. Other than a few phone calls discussing arrangements for their daughter's wedding, he'd given Alexa the space she needed. But today was the day he'd been living for.

The second he rang the bell, Alexa opened the door and came out on the porch looking anxious. She'd dressed in jeans and a sleeveless top, telling him what he'd feared, but it didn't surprise him.

"What happened to your promise?" he asked without preamble.

She rubbed her hands over womanly hips

in a nervous gesture. "We can't do this, Nico. You know we can't."

"Did you tell your grandfather our plans?"

Alexa averted her eyes. "I haven't said anything yet."

"Then *I* will because the priest is expecting us in less than three hours, and I refuse to marry you without receiving Gavril's blessing."

"He won't give it, Nico."

"I think he will, Alexa. Admit it's what we both want."

"You know I do, but I'm nervous."

Nico waited until she turned and went inside. He followed her into the living room. "I'll wait here while you find him."

After one more worried glance at him, she disappeared. Nico walked around looking at framed pictures of her family. He caught sight of one taken of him and his daughter the night of the announcement dinner at his villa. He picked it up to study it. Nico had put his arm around Dimitra while they smiled at each other. His heart melted just looking at it.

"Well, Nico." Alexa had wheeled her grandfather into the room. He smiled at him. "I didn't know you were coming over this morning. Phyllis was just fixing me breakfast. You look like you're going to a wedding." Nico had come dressed for the occasion in a navy dress suit and tie.

He put the picture back on the table. "I am. Last week I asked Alexa to marry me and planned it for today. We'll be taking our vows at the church in Sarti at noon with Anna and Thanos for witnesses. But no marriage can take place until we have your blessing. I owe you more than you will ever know."

The older man looked at his granddaughter in surprise. When she didn't say anything Nico explained, "We didn't want to intrude on Dimitra's big day, so we've decided to marry in private. It's what we want and need. Only *you* and my friend Irena are privy to our news. I'll bring Alexa back here by the end of the day. Once our daughter and Kristos return from their honeymoon, we'll tell them and announce our marriage to the world."

He didn't have to wait long for Gavril to grasp Alexa's hand. The gesture shot relief through Nico. Gavril eyed his granddaughter. "Why aren't you ready, sweetheart?"

"You mean you're happy about it?" The fear and disbelief in her voice made Nico want to wrap her in his arms and never let her go. She'd suffered guilt for too long. Since Raisa's death no one understood what guilt could do to you more than Nico did. But now that Alexa had come back into his life, he'd made up his mind they both needed to rid themselves of those chains.

Gavril gave a gruff chuckle. "I've only prayed for it for nineteen years." By the look on her face, his remark had stunned her. "Go on. Wear that pretty dress you wore the night you went to meet Kristos's mother."

"You won't need anything else," Nico murmured.

"Hurry, sweetheart. You don't want to be late for your own wedding."

At her grandfather's admonition, she left the room.

Nico walked over to Gavril and clasped his hand. "I swear I'll love your granddaughter forever. I'm also making another promise to take care of you for the rest of your life."

The older man's eyes filled. He wiped away the moisture as Alexa came back in the living room and kissed her grandfather. She wore the blue-on-white-print dress and carried a handbag. "You're right. It's what I've always dreamed of."

Nico helped her out to the car and drove them to headquarters. En route he turned to her. "You look heavenly."

"Thank you. You look wonderful too. But Nico...there's something I haven't told you." Her voice shook.

"What? That you can't have any more children? Because if you can't, we'll adopt."

"No. I'm talking about my grandfather."

"While you were getting dressed, I told him I'd take care of him to the end of his days."

"But you don't understand. He needs me. Once Dimitra is married, he'll be too lonely. I could never leave him."

"You won't have to. I'll be your husband and plan to move in with you."

She stared at him in utter astonishment. "You have your own home."

"We'll have the villa in Sarti for a getaway and to entertain. You can be sure that Kristos and Dimitra will use it a lot. But now that we're getting married, my permanent home will be with you. I'll move in while the love-birds are on their honeymoon. Gavril has taken care of you all these years. Now it's my turn to help him."

"I would never expect that of you, Nico."

"But I want to. Think what he did for me while I wasn't there. Naturally your grandfather is the most comfortable in his own home with Phyllis taking care of him. It's centrally located for friends who want to come by and visit. It's close to my work and the university where you teach. That's the way our life will be while I do all I can for you and your family."

Alexa broke down sobbing, the last reaction he'd expected.

"What have I said that has upset you so much?" By now they'd reached headquarters.

She wiped her eyes with the backs of her hands. "I'm not upset. I'm just overawed by your kindness to my grandfather."

"He's a remarkable man, and we're going to do everything right this time. A new chapter of life is starting, and we're not in our dotage yet. First we'll become man and wife as we'd planned ages ago."

"But I might not conceive." In desperation she cried, "If we do go through with this wedding, then I want you to give me your solemn promise about something."

"What's that?"

"If I haven't become pregnant within four months, then you'll move back to your villa. We'll get a quiet divorce so you can find a woman to marry who can give you a child. It's what you want and I refuse to stand in your way."

He turned off the engine and turned to her, giving her a penetrating glance. "Since I got you pregnant the first time we made love,

I'm willing to bet the same thing will happen again, so I'll make you that promise."

Alexa couldn't believe it. "Y-you mean it?" she asked in a shaky voice.

"I always mean what I say, but four months doesn't give us much time. Just so you understand. If you are pregnant in four months' time, we'll stay together forever. I want your promise *you* won't back out."

"Of course I won't. You're teasing me again."

"You think?"

"I *know.*"

He laughed before opening the door. "Now that we've cleared the air, we need to go. My pilot is waiting to fly us to Sithonia."

The flight to Sithonia presented breathtaking images of the mountains and greenery. It gave a different perspective than driving there. Alexa sat behind the pilot while she marveled over the scenery from the helicopter.

"You've found paradise here, Nico. I can well understand why you settled here."

He looked over his shoulder at her. "Would you believe I had you in mind when I bought it? Though I never expected to see you again, the private beach seemed to have a certain mermaid's name written on it."

His words melted her heart. "Yet you're willing to live in my grandfather's home so we can be together."

"We'll get away on weekends. Perhaps the time will come when he'll want to live in the villa too. You never know what the future will bring."

Darling Nico. After he'd learned he had a daughter, he wanted another child to replace the one he'd lost when his wife had died. He'd suffered a great loss.

The fact that he was willing to go through all this with Alexa proved that he'd truly loved his wife and had looked forward to the birth of their child. Not knowing of Dimitra's existence, his need for that unfulfilled dream had gone much deeper than Alexa had realized. It explained why he was anxious to marry Alexa and have a baby.

Alexa couldn't promise she would be pregnant that soon. But she would try to give him what he wanted because she loved him heart and soul. If it gave Nico any hope, then she was willing because she realized his suffering had been infinite. No one had a stronger will than Nico, yet not even *his* will could guarantee such an outcome.

Thanos and Anna met them at the villa in an estate car. After she freshened up, they were driven to the charming Church of the Assumption in the village. The tan exterior with painted red facings featured a belfry with a cross. Nico helped her out and cupped her elbow. "Are you ready?"

Alexa didn't know what she was and couldn't answer.

"We're simply going to exchange vows. The ceremony will be short. The priest knows we fell in love as teenagers and he's happy to be officiating."

Anxious, she looked up. "Does he—"

"No," Nico cut her off, reading her mind.

"He only knows Dimitra is our daughter, nothing else. Shall we go inside?"

It was too late to back out now, not that she wanted to. They walked up the few steps into the foyer. Beyond the inner doors the narrow nave extended to the icons of saints erected at the front of the chapel. The older priest in his robes stood smiling at them.

Nico led her up the aisle. Anna and Thanos sat on the chairs in front to witness the ceremony.

"Kyría Remis? It is my pleasure to meet the woman Kýrie Angelis has chosen to marry. If you'll join hands, we'll begin."

She glanced at Nico, who'd never looked more gorgeous wearing a navy dress suit to die for. It didn't seem possible that this was going to happen. Of course this was what she'd always wanted, but not quite in this way. So rushed and secretive.

He took hold of her hand and threaded his fingers through hers, giving them a squeeze as if he could read her mind.

The priest said a prayer, then looked at

Nico. "Nicholas Timon Angelis, do you take this woman to be your lawfully wedded wife? To love her, provide for her in sickness and in health until death do you part?"

"I do," he answered in his deep voice.

That was so short, Alexa couldn't believe it. This ceremony was nothing like a normal Greek one. She swallowed hard as the priest stared at her. "Alexa Soriano Remis, do you take this man to be your lawfully wedded husband? To love him, support him through sickness and health until death do you part?"

The priest didn't know about the four-month time limit she'd forced Nico to honor. "I do."

"Then in as much as the two of you have plighted your troth, I hereby pronounce you man and wife, in the name of the Father, the Son and the Holy Spirit. You may exchange rings now."

Nico reached in his breast pocket and brought out a ring with a dazzling green stone set in gold he slid on to her ring finger. Alexa hadn't bought him a ring because she'd never thought she'd marry him. But before she'd left the house, she'd grabbed the engaged-to-be-engaged gold ring he'd sent her in his first letter.

She removed it from the finger on her right hand and reached for his left hand. It only slid partway on to his pinky finger. He recognized it at once, flashing her an all-consuming glance she couldn't decipher.

"Congratulations. You may now kiss your bride, Kýrie Angelis."

The brief kiss Nico gave her was almost as surprising as the shortest marriage service performed in Greek history. Had this ceremony been such a painful reminder of his first marriage, he couldn't wait for it to be over?

Alexa didn't know what to think as he led her to the foyer where Thanos and Anna congratulated them. The priest followed and asked them to sign the marriage document.

With that over, Nico ushered her outside to the car. Thanos drove them back to the villa. When they entered the villa, Nico guided her to the patio.

"Anna is serving us lunch out here."

They sat beneath the umbrella. There was no sign of an eager young bridegroom so anxious to be with his new bride that food was the last thing on his mind.

He poured them wine while Anna brought the food. "Our ceremony had to be shortened. The priest texted me during the flight that he needed to leave on an emergency, and we arrived there later than planned."

That was the reason? "I didn't realize, but I didn't mind it being short."

"Believe me. Neither did I. It has given us more time to enjoy the rest of the day until we have to fly back."

Alexa had lost her appetite, but she didn't want to insult Anna, so she ate as much of the crab salad as she could handle and thanked her. Nico, on the other hand, ate two sandwiches along with salad.

She looked at her wedding ring. "This teardrop stone is dazzling. What kind is it?"

"A natural deep green diamond, very rare. It came from a mine in Africa. I bought it a week ago. It symbolizes harmony, freshness and fertility, the color of nature. The color of your eyes."

She looked away, unable to meet his piercing gaze.

"I didn't really believe you meant to marry me today. I'm sorry I didn't have a ring for you."

"But you did," he came back and held up his left hand. "I'm pleased to see you found this ring in that first letter."

"I was so moved when I read what was engraved on it, I fell apart. It's been sitting in my jewelry box."

"But no longer." He got up from the table. "Why don't we go to my bedroom so I can put it on you officially."

Alexa's heart thudded so violently, it was hard to breathe. She stood and followed Nico to another part of the villa, halting in the doorway of his spacious bedroom with its king-size bed.

The shutters had been closed to darken the room. She could smell the fragrance of orange blossoms. Candles had been lit and placed on the dresser and end tables. A huge plant of blue hydrangeas sat on a coffee table in front of two matching love seats.

"Nico—" she gasped and rested against the doorjamb. "I feel like I've entered the cabin on your cruiser and it's nineteen years ago."

"That was a night I'll never forget," he murmured. "If you'd like to freshen up first, the en suite bathroom is through that door. I've put a blue robe on a hook for you."

Her legs felt insubstantial as she thanked him and walked across the room to his private bathroom. With trembling hands she removed her clothes and took a shower, but all her actions seemed to be in slow motion. Alexa couldn't believe she was now a married woman. This was her wedding night, even if it was early afternoon.

How different from the first time when he'd carried her to the bed in his cabin below deck. Until they'd had to leave the cruiser, she hadn't thought about anything but loving him.

Alexa started to be afraid. She had been with other men and thoroughly kissed, but she hadn't made love since that night with Nico. What if he found her less than satisfactory, especially after his marriage to a young Raisa.

After leaving the shower, she used one of the fluffy towels to dry off, then slipped on the blue toweling robe. Alexa glanced in the mirror, not thrilled with the sight of the thirty-six-year-old woman who looked back at her.

Last week Alexa had finally broken down and done a search of his deceased wife online. She'd been absolutely beautiful, a tall Athenian with flowing black hair and velvety brown eyes. Anyone would think she modeled for a living.

Alexa found photo after photo of the famous couple, including wedding pictures at the church in Athens. Nico had seemed so happy, but when information about the helicopter crash came up on the screen, she'd shut it off unable to go there. It hurt too much to imagine the pain he must have gone through.

"Alexa? Are you all right?"

She'd been so deep in thought, she hadn't heard the tap on the door.

"I'm fine, Nico. I'll be right out."

When she emerged, she found him waiting for her dressed in a black striped robe, looking the heart-stopping male she adored. He walked over and reached for her left hand. "This ring belongs with your wedding ring, Kyría Angelis." He slid the ring he'd been wearing on his pinky to her finger. "You're my wife now."

"I never thought this day would come."

He put his hands on her shoulders and looked into her eyes. "Another miracle. Now tell me what's wrong."

She looked everywhere except at him. "If you want to know the truth, I'm nervous."

"Why?" That wicked half smile of his was in evidence. "It isn't as if we haven't done this before."

"That's true, but it's been a long time."

"Then come over on the bed and we'll talk about it."

"I'm afraid."

"Of me?"

"Yes!"

"You've known me better than anyone else has ever known me."

"That's why I'm terrified!"

He laughed that deep, rich male laugh she loved before he picked her up in his arms and carried her to the bed. Then he rolled on his side next to her and kissed her mouth. "Even if the priest had an emergency, you need to know I didn't kiss you the way I wanted to at the church because I knew if I did, I'd never stop."

"Even if that's not the truth, thank you for saying it."

The sheen faded from his eyes. "What's going on with you?"

"Nothing. I'm sorry."

"You had a reason for saying that. Talk to me, Alexa."

She took a deep breath. "You've been married. Today probably reminded you of your wedding to Raisa. I could understand why it was hard for you to kiss me at the altar."

"You couldn't be more wrong." He sounded upset.

"Are you saying she's never on your mind?"

"I'm saying that when I do think about her, it's more to do with the crash I couldn't prevent."

"But it wasn't your fault."

"That's true, but the guilt lingers."

"Of course it does, and I'm sorry I brought her up. I guess I'm feeling terribly insecure. You have to understand this is all new to me."

Nico raised up on his elbow. "Are you saying you never slept with those two men you almost married?"

"No. After what happened to me, I vowed I'd never sleep with a man unless we were married first. No matter what, I couldn't risk the possibility of another pregnancy."

He looked down at her, cradling her head in his hand. His gaze wandered over every feature. "I know Dimitra has brought you joy, but you've suffered too. We need each other," he said against her mouth.

Suddenly this was the old Nico, kissing her as if it were life to him. They slowly gave each other kiss for kiss, savoring the taste and feel of each other. He might not be in love with her anymore and couldn't say the words, but their hunger said the powerful physical attraction they felt hadn't faded with time.

"I can't believe you're my wife and we're married at last." He kissed every part of her face and throat. "Our last night together on the cruiser was painful for me because I knew I'd be leaving you for a year. You don't know how close I came to kidnapping you."

"You don't mean it." She searched his eyes.

"I'm ashamed to say I had it all planned. Instead of going to work earlier that day, I loaded the cruiser with extra petrol and food for our getaway to Turkey. Once we arrived there I had contacts who would arrange for us to fly to South America undercover."

"You're kidding—" she cried. "Why didn't you? I would have gone anywhere with you."

"I know you would have. That's how much I believed in your love. But after making love to you, guilt and reason held me back. You weren't quite eighteen yet. If we'd been caught, I would have been sentenced in a court of law for disappearing with a minor and avoiding military service.

"Not even my family would have been able to protect me and I'd lose you forever while I went to prison. The thought of years of separation from you was anathema to me. At the last moment my sanity returned. I realized I would have to wait a year for you in order to get what I wanted, but I knew it would be worth it."

Tears filled her eyes. "Instead I'm the one who kept us apart for years."

He kissed away the moisture. "Hush. Right now all I want is to make love to you. Do you know you're even more beautiful than ever? I came close to a heart attack when you walked out on Irena's patio."

She buried her face in his neck. "I had one

when I saw you on TV for the first time. You'll never know."

"But I do." He found her mouth and they began to devour each other. Every touch and caress created such rapture, she found herself in a world of ecstasy she never wanted to end. All the years she'd missed being with him like this no longer mattered. She was in his arms now, knowing a passion that had her spiraling.

Alexa clung to him, relishing the sheer joy of being alive and knowing his possession. How she'd lived this long without him, she couldn't comprehend. They were so hungry for each other, she lost cognizance of time. It was as if they were trying to make up for all the years of deprivation and couldn't stop.

She couldn't get enough of him. It was almost embarrassing how on fire she was, especially when she groaned aloud after his cell phone rang. The sound forced them to get unentangled enough for him to answer it, but their legs were still entwined. She lay back, trying to catch her breath.

The candles had burned down almost all the way. They had to have been making love for a long time for that to happen. She heard a short conversation before Nico leaned over and gave her a long, insatiable kiss. "That was Thanos. Would you believe it's after eight? The pilot was ready to take us back three hours ago."

"Oh, no. I need to get home. I promised my grandfather."

"Don't worry. He knows where we are and what we're doing."

"Nico—" A wave of heat engulfed her body. Inside she wanted to cry out in frustration. To have to leave her husband's arms was the greatest torture she could imagine.

His deep laughter was the final insult. "I'll phone him and let him know we're going to be late. I doubt he expects us at all."

"But Dimitra will wonder if I get home after she does."

"Would that be such a terrible thing?"

"I don't want her to know we're married yet." Somehow she managed to elude Nico's arms and reached for her robe lying on the floor. "I'll get showered and dressed."

"Don't plan to run away from me this fast again," he warned against her neck before letting her go. It sent delicious shivers through her.

CHAPTER TEN

WHEN ALEXA CAME out of the bathroom a few minutes later, she discovered Nico had already showered and dressed, this time in a sport shirt and chinos. His eyes were dark fires of desire before he extinguished the candles. "You must know the last thing I want to do is leave here."

"I feel the same way." But if she bared her soul completely, she'd blurt out her love for him, a love that had never died. Would he be able to say the same thing back? She didn't know, but prayed she was already pregnant. Alexa had conceived on the cruiser. Why not now, or in the next four months? She wanted to believe it.

Alexa wasn't the same woman who'd walked in his mountain villa after their wedding ceremony earlier in the day. Nico had made her his wife in every sense of the word. She had to be the envy of any woman who'd ever laid eyes on him and wanted a relationship with him.

Nico would never know how hard it was for her to leave this idyllic place. For a little while she'd been able to pretend that he loved her as he'd once done. Was she wrong and he did have those intense feelings for her even if he hadn't said the words?

The sound of whirring rotors broke into her thoughts before they approached the helicopter. Nico helped her inside, giving her hip a possessive squeeze before she found her seat and he strapped her in.

"We'll be there soon." Nico lowered his mouth to give her a heart-stopping kiss before he climbed in front and put on his headset. As they rose in the air, he looked over his broad shoulder at her. His dark eyes were alive with a light she hadn't seen in nineteen years.

He hoped he'd already made her pregnant.

No one wanted that to happen more than she did.

A glint from her diamond caught her eye. Much as she hated to do it, she put both rings in her purse. That was all Dimitra would have to see. Even if she would be happy with the news. Deep down Alexa wanted their marriage more than anything, but didn't want their news to take away from their daughter's wedding day.

Once the helicopter touched down at Angelis headquarters, Nico helped her down and they rushed to his car for the drive home.

"Tomorrow let's meet for lunch at 7 Thalasses with Dimitra and Kristos. We'll eat outside. They have excellent seafood."

She shot him a glance. "Which you love."

"So do you."

Alexa smiled. "I admit it."

He reached over to clasp her hand. "Let's ask Gavril and Irena to join us so we can wrap up any details for the wedding."

His warmth crept through her body. "I'm

glad you suggested it. Irena and I need to put our heads together."

"I'll call her. After we drive Gavril back to the house tomorrow, we'll slip away to my apartment above the office for a few hours. That's one time when no one will be around to notice."

"Let's hope." Just the thought of being in his arms again created so much excitement, her heart thumped too hard to be healthy.

When they drew up to the house, she saw no sign of Kristos's car. Nico walked her to the door and checked his watch. "It's ten to eleven. Our daughter probably isn't home yet."

"I'm not sure."

Nico pulled her in his arms and kissed her passionately before letting her go. "I'll be by for you at noon. I don't know about you, but it's going to be an endless night for me without you." On that note he walked back to the car and drove off.

You don't know the half of it, Nico Angelis.

* * *

Later Nico had only just entered his apartment when his phone rang. He grabbed it, thinking it had to be Alexa. Their wedding day had been cut short by having to leave the villa. To be forced to say good-night at her grandfather's door when he'd needed the rest of the night to make love to her had come close to killing him. If she felt the same way, maybe she'd changed her mind and wanted him to come and get her right now. With a pounding heart he checked the caller ID.

Disappointment flooded his system before he clicked on. "Giannina? What's going on?" She'd never called him this late, and this was definitely not the time for a conversation.

"Can I drive over and talk to you in private?"

She sounded on the verge of panic. It was totally unlike her. "Can't we do this over the phone?"

"No. I have to show you something. It's an emergency."

He frowned. "All right. How soon can you get here?"

"Five minutes."

"I'll wait for you out in front and we can talk in your car."

"Thank heaven for you, Nico."

"Giannina, whatever is going on, it couldn't be that bad."

"You want to make a bet?" The line went dead.

Nico needed a glass of water, then he rode the elevator down to the lobby. He nodded to Gus and walked outside to wait for his sister. She drove her dark red Lexus LC overspeed most of the time. Tonight was no different as she screeched to a halt in front of the entrance.

He opened the door and got in. "Drive around the side where we won't be noticed."

Within a minute Giannina pulled to a stop and shut off the engine. She reached in the backseat and handed him a mock-up copy of the *Halkidiki News*. "This will be out in the morning. Read the headline. It has been attributed to me of course." She turned on the map light for him.

Lost Royal Heir of Hellenia Found Alive!

Nico's head reared. "*You* broke this story? With civil war close to breaking out in Hellenia, this has to be the biggest news to hit Europe in years."

"It's a lie of the worst kind, Nico. You know as well as I do Prince Alexandros disappeared a long time ago and has never been seen again. Since I'm the managing editor, I'll be blamed for spreading a story that has no proof. Someone on the inside wants me gone from the newspaper and caused it to be printed without my authority. I know who it is."

Nico was afraid he did too. "You're talking about Uncle Ari." The man held dual citizenship and spent a lot of his time in Hellenia. Who knew what was going on inside him?

"He has staffers who are loyal to him and would do something this monstrous behind my back."

"You're right. Where is Ari now?"

"Probably at the newspaper."

"Then I'll go over there now. After I get a confession out of him, I'll force him to print a disclaimer before I fire him. Our father should have done it years ago."

"Thank heaven for you, brother dear." She reached over to hug him hard. "I don't know what I'd do without you, Nico." Giannina wiped her eyes. "I'm sorry. I've only been talking about my problems. How's Dimitra?"

"Wonderful. I'll tell you about her later. Now I've got to go. If I don't find him at the office, I'll track him at home, then I'll call you to let you know what happened."

He got out of her car and walked around the building to reach his car. But before he did anything else, he needed to hear his wife's voice and know today wasn't a dream. Then he'd drive to the newspaper and confront their uncle.

Saturday after lunch, where more plans for the wedding were pinned down, Nico drove Alexa and Gavril back to the house. With

Phyllis there, Alexa didn't need to worry about leaving her grandfather for a few hours.

Before they left for his apartment, she heard Nico ask her grandfather some questions about the political climate in Hellenia, of all things. She wondered why. Her two favorite men had admired each other from the beginning and were more alike than they knew, a fact that thrilled Alexa.

When Nico walked her out to the car and they drove to his apartment, she asked him about it.

"I wanted to pick his brains. That man knows more about what goes on than anyone in the government."

He kissed her senseless on the ride up in the elevator. But when they stepped into his luxurious apartment, she turned to him. "What aren't you telling me?"

Nico picked her up and carried her into the bedroom, following her down on the bed. "I promise to reveal all, but not yet. I've been living to be alone with you and don't want to waste a second of it."

After his late phone call last night to say good-night, Alexa had almost said she'd leave the house and come to him. Their wedding night had been cut short. She'd ached for him all through the rest of the night and had to suppress her feelings during lunch. But there was no holding back now.

They knew how to bring each other pleasure beyond description. He swept her away on a new tide of passion that left both of them breathless. No woman wanting to conceive had ever had a lover like Nico.

Already she knew she'd been out of her mind to put a four-month limit on their marriage. She wanted to tell him she didn't mean it. She needed to tell him how deeply in love she was with him and always had been. Only one thing held her back.

There was no torrent of words about his love for her. She could wait, but he couldn't say them. While he lay there asleep with his arm hugging her hip possessively, she studied his striking male features, the lines of his compelling mouth. No other man had been created so divinely. It almost hurt to look at him he was so perfect to her.

"Alexa?" Nico had awakened and brushed the tears off her cheeks. "What's wrong?"

It was too late to hide emotions erupting inside her. "I've been reliving those early years when I didn't understand why I'd never heard from you. We'd been so happy, then suddenly it was all over."

"Tell me about it." He pulled her into his arms, crushing her against him. "But don't let it torture you. We're together now."

"We are!" She burrowed her face in his neck. More tears spilled out on his shoulder. "Do you remember that last Saturday years ago when we flew to Olympia?"

He kissed her hair. "How could I ever forget?"

"I told you how much I loved the Greek myths and you took me to the Olympia archaeological museum for a surprise. That was the first time I'd seen the statue of the life-size Hermes sculpted by the ancient sculptor Praxiteles. It had been done in that beautiful

Paros marble. He was carrying the baby Dionysus to the Nysiades, the mythical nymphs of Mount Nysa."

Nico rolled her over so he could look into her eyes. "I said you bore a strong resemblance to the painting of the young, gorgeous nymph Erato who helped take care of him."

She nodded. Alexa never forgot anything he'd said to her. "Something happened to me when I saw that statue, but I didn't tell you at the time."

"What was that?" He kissed the end of her nose.

"We'd been talking about getting married and having a family. That statue reminded me of you. There was a look of such tenderness and fascination on his face as he held the baby in his arm. It was a brilliant work of art that stayed with me. I could imagine you carrying our baby like that one day, but I never dreamed that I'd be pregnant before you went away. You should have had the opportunity to raise our little Dimitra."

"Alexa..." He ran a hand through her hair. "Why are you still agonizing over that?"

"I can't help it. When I think of the years she missed out knowing your love and how fun you are. There's no one more exciting than you. Didn't you notice at lunch today how she wanted to talk to you the whole time? You light up her world. I've never seen her this happy in my life. I'm sure Kristos has seen a big difference in her. Irena remarked on it to me before they drove away from the restaurant."

"I've never been happier either."

"That's the problem, Nico."

"What do you mean?"

She couldn't look at him. "I know you want a baby so badly and are so excited about it."

"But you aren't?"

"You know I am, but I'm afraid I might not be able to get pregnant. I talked to my OB here in Salonica the other day. He said that from the ages of twenty-five to thirty-six you have an eighty-six percent chance of conception if you keep trying at the fertile time."

"I'll take those odds considering we won't miss any of your fertile days."

Oh, Nico. "But the odds aren't the same as they were when I was seventeen. He also reminded me that it's harder to stay pregnant if you do conceive."

"Let's take it one problem at a time. Right now we don't have any. In fact I don't believe we're in any hurry to get you home."

"Don't joke about this, Nico. Four months might not be long enough. I don't want you to have to wait another second beyond that time before you find another woman who can give you children."

His eyes wandered over her. "We've already had this conversation and have produced the perfect child together. You're young and I don't anticipate any problems. Now let's stop talking."

Within seconds he'd covered her mouth with his own and set her on fire as only he could do. She lost all sense of time while they found ways to bring each other pleasure. Nico created ecstasy beyond comprehension.

It was dark outside by the time she stirred and eased away from him.

"Where do you think you're going?"

"To the bathroom for a shower. I need to get back home."

He drew her back against him. "What if I ask you to stay the night with me?"

She wanted that more than he knew. "If we're trying to keep our marriage a secret, then it wouldn't be a good idea."

Nico pulled her closer. "The thing is, tomorrow I have to go out of town on important business. I might be gone several days and am not certain when I'll be back."

That shouldn't have upset her. "Where are you going?"

"Not far."

She frowned, sensing he was keeping something from her. "You can't tell your own wife?" she teased.

"I promise to tell you everything after I return."

Suddenly the idea that he was leaving Salonica for any reason at all frightened her.

The last time he'd flown away from her, he'd never come back. It was silly of her to be this worried, but she couldn't help it. "I've a feeling this doesn't have anything to do with your work."

"My lips are sealed for now."

Alexa knew it, and didn't like the sound of it. But she didn't want to behave like a nagging wife. Instead, she slid out of his arms and hurried across the room to the bathroom.

Twenty minutes later he walked her to the door of her grandfather's home. She could tell he was preoccupied. "I'll text you when I can." After a hungry kiss, he walked swiftly to his car. Naturally there were no words of love from him.

How long are you going to wait for something that's never going to happen, Alexa? How long do you think you can play house with him, knowing the most important ingredient for you is missing?

It took all her self-control to keep from crying out her love for him. If she did, she'd never stop.

* * *

Over the next two days, Alexa lost a lot of sleep. Until she heard from Nico, she knew she wouldn't be able to accomplish anything. On Wednesday morning she was so anxious, she had no desire to go on her morning run. It wouldn't help her.

Dimitra had just left the house for the university with Kristos. Her daughter had no reason to be concerned that her father was away on business. Alexa went into the kitchen to make coffee, all the while waiting for her husband's call. She could hear her grandfather talking to Phyllis while he was getting dressed. It might be a normal day, but it didn't feel like one.

While she was pouring coffee into a mug, her phone rang, causing her to spill some on the counter. She grabbed her cell without looking at the caller ID. "Nico—" she cried.

"No. It's Giannina."

"Oh—" She gripped it tighter in disappointment. "Hi. How are you?" They hadn't talked since Alexa had gone to lunch with her.

"Alexa, it's obvious you haven't heard the news. Nico left town for me on a secret mission."

What?

"In the middle of last night he was in a car on his way home with some NIS agents when there was a collision."

Alexa's cry brought her grandfather and Phyllis into the kitchen. She thought she was going to faint and sat on the nearest chair. "H-he isn't—"

"He's alive."

"Oh, thank heaven, thank heaven."

"Everyone survived, but Nico was brought to Saint Paul Hospital unconscious and still is. I don't know the extent of his injuries. My parents and I are here with him, waiting for news from the doctor about his condition."

Alexa tried to stifle a moan, but she wasn't successful. She feared for Nico's father with his heart problem.

"Is Dimitra there? I know this news is going to come as a horrible shock to her."

Dimitra... This was agony beyond bearing. "No. Kristos came by and they've gone to the university."

"Then he doesn't know either. I'll phone Irena. She'll want to be told and get in touch with her son. She adores my brother."

We all adore him.

A groan came out of Alexa. "I—I'll text Dimitra," she stammered. "She'll tell Kristos." It was a struggle for breath. "What floor are you on?"

"Six. We're in the lounge area, east wing."

"I'll be there soon." She hung up.

Her grandfather wheeled his chair next to her. "What terrible news has caused you to go white as a sheet?"

"Oh, Papoú—" She threw her arms around him. "It's Nico. He was in a car crash last night and hasn't gained consciousness yet. I've got to get to Saint Paul Hospital, and Dimitra has to be told."

"You leave that to me. I'll call her while you get dressed. We'll all go and pick her up on our way to the hospital. He needs his family with him."

Alexa didn't remember getting dressed or driving to the hospital with her grandfather and Phyllis. Irena had already called Kristos. He was bringing Dimitra straight from the university.

Within a half hour, a congregation had gathered in the lounge area, everyone waiting to hear from the doctor. Alexa couldn't sit still and kept watching for any sign of someone to come and tell them what was going on.

How could this have happened after all the suffering Nico had been through in his life? It wasn't fair. He was the best man on earth. She looked around the room. Everyone loved and needed him. He held their world together.

Though they'd been separated all those years, Alexa had always known where she could find Nico. But if the worst happened to him now, there was no address on earth she could look up to find him.

The second she saw a nurse come in the lounge, Alexa ran up to her. "Do you have news about Kýrie Angelis?"

"The doctor will be in shortly to talk to

everyone," she said before walking over to Nico's parents.

Dimitra ran over and put an arm around her waist. "What did she tell you?"

"Nothing. She said to wait for the doctor."

"I don't believe Baba is going to die. We just found each other."

Alexa hugged her around the shoulders. "I agree. He's going to pull out of this and walk you down the aisle. You'll see." Her daughter was trying valiantly not to break down. Alexa needed to be strong for her. "We have to have faith." More faith than Alexa had exhibited in her entire life.

A few minutes after the nurse left the lounge, the doctor came in and headed straight for Nico's parents. She clung to Dimitra while they waited to hear the news.

"The good news is Kýrie Angelis has awakened. He has cuts and bruises, but it's his head that was impacted by the crash." Dimitra broke down quietly, hugging Alexa. "We've run scans to know if there's been significant damage to the brain. We'll have the results soon."

"Can I go in?" his mother asked in a tear-filled voice.

"No one is allowed to see him yet. Since he came to, he has asked repeatedly for us to send in his wife."

Upon hearing that, Alexa's heart almost jumped out of her chest.

"It's an indication that he's lost some of his memory. Whether it's temporary or permanent, we won't know for a while."

Alexa took a deep breath. "He hasn't lost his memory, doctor."

Everyone looked at Alexa as if she'd lost her mind.

"I'm his wife."

A collective gasp resounded in the room. Dimitra looked at her in shock.

"We were married in a private ceremony at the church in Sarti Village the other day, and planned to tell all of you after Dimitra and Kristos were married. But circumstances have changed the timeline." He had to love her a bit to want to see her before anyone else, right? "May I see him now?"

"Of course," the doctor murmured. "Come with me."

"Go to him, Mama." With stars in her eyes, Dimitra gave her a hard hug before letting her go.

Nico prayed he wasn't hallucinating when Alexa came in the room and walked over to his bedside. She wore a filmy pale blue sundress with spaghetti straps. He had a royal headache, but there was nothing wrong with his vision. Her gorgeous face had a pallor that told him how she'd been suffering.

"Darling—" She finally said the word he'd been waiting for. Her sea-green eyes filled with liquid. "I had to tell them I was your wife, or they wouldn't have let me see you before anyone else. Everyone loves you so terribly and is clamoring to see that you are all right."

He lifted the hand that didn't have an IV so she would take hold of it. "Thank heaven our secret is out. I couldn't have lived with it another second. Don't you know I want to shout it to the world that we're together forever? *Agape mou.* I love you to the depth of my soul. Kiss me."

"Are you sure it's all right?" She sounded so frightened.

"Would you rather I expired while I wait for it?"

"Oh, Nico—I'm so in love with you, it hurts." She leaned over and gave him the kiss of life. Her shiny chestnut hair fell around them.

When she finally lifted her head he said, "As the car met head-on with the other car, I couldn't believe I had to say goodbye to my beloved again. I couldn't bear it and called on the powers that be to perform a miracle."

"It's more than a miracle," she cried softly. "You're not only alive, you're completely yourself. I'm overjoyed. I love you, Nico."

"I've been dying to hear those words from you. I knew that if you said them, it meant you'd gotten over your guilt from the past."

"I have, and I'll keep telling you I love you till you're sick of it. You have no idea how much I love you. Are you really feeling all right?"

"Other than a headache, I've never felt this wonderful."

"That's the kind of news I like to hear," a male voice intruded. The doctor had come in the room and walked over to them. "Your tests are back. No permanent damage has been done. I'm keeping you here until tomorrow morning. If all is well, then you'll be released. And by the way, congratulations on your marriage."

"Thank you, Doctor."

"I'll give your families the good news, but I don't want you bombarded with visitors."

"I'll make sure he doesn't overdo it," Alexa assured him.

As the doctor left the room, Nico squeezed her hand. "The minute I'm released, we're going to fly to the villa and spend a few days alone. We need it in the worst way."

"Nico—" She laughed. "Now I know you're

back to normal I need to tell our daughter she doesn't have to worry. Be good while I go get her."

"Don't leave me yet. I need another kiss."

"So do I, my love." She kissed him one more time before leaving his room.

Less than a minute passed before Dimitra appeared. "Baba—" She leaned over to hug him carefully. "I'm so thankful you and Mama are married. I love you more than you will ever know."

"You took the words out of my mouth."

Life didn't get better than this.

CHAPTER ELEVEN

THOUGH THEY'D FLOWN to Sarti on Thursday, it was Nico who drove them down to his private beach in the estate car on Friday. Another glorious, hot July day greeted them.

Other than a few bruises on his right upper arm and thigh, you would never have known he'd escaped death in a car crash. There was a little cut at the corner of his right eyebrow, and another one on his right earlobe, but those would fade.

Nico was still Alexa's fantasy. In fact she would love to hire a sculptor who would create a statue of him, but no work of art could ever match the wonder of him in the flesh. She told him that as they ran out in the turquoise water. Farther on it turned a deeper blue.

"A statue of me?" He laughed his head off.

Another wonderful quality of his was the fact that he wasn't in love with himself. No other man had more reason to think otherwise. Not Nico. He was perfect.

"Yes. I'll have it erected in the backyard and go out to look at you while you're at work."

He'd gone out deeper and was treading water while she swam to him. "How about we have a statue of you erected and put in the front yard. Everyone who comes to your grandfather's house will see the exotic mermaid and fall madly in love with her."

"I'm afraid I don't look like I did at seventeen and can't stand the scrutiny."

He flashed her a devilish smile. "I happen to think you're more breathtaking than ever and can't wait to see you pregnant. It's a sight I've been waiting for since you told me Dimitra was our daughter. Wouldn't it be something if the two of you ended up expecting babies at the same time?"

"I don't wish that on her yet. They're still young."

They circled each other. "I don't know,

Alexa. After the way I've seen our lives turn out so far, I've stopped thinking about what we should or shouldn't do. Life is a gift and we need to welcome it."

"You're right, darling. She and Kristos have found each other, and their wedding day will be here soon enough. Imagine if you become a father and a grandfather at the same time."

"I *have* been thinking about it. Our *papoú* will be a great-great-grandfather."

For Nico to call her grandfather *our papoú* meant their world had come full circle and they were a family in every sense of the word. She loved Nico so much she did a somersault and wrapped her arms around his hips, pulling him under the water.

They played like children, relishing in the joy of being together. After a time Nico got serious. He carried her out of the water to the beach and lowered her to one of his big beach towels laid out on the fine sand.

His dark eyes burned with desire. "I'm going to make love to you, my wife, right under a blazing sun."

She smiled at him. "What took you so long? I've been waiting for you to fulfill the promise you made me before your accident."

"You mean about making up for the time we had to spend apart? I hope you're ready."

"Is there any question I'm not?" She rolled over on top of him and began kissing every feature of his handsome face. He kissed her back. For the next little while they forgot everything except loving each other into oblivion.

"I wanted to do this the first day we met nineteen years ago," she admitted later when the sun was in a different part of the sky. "I hated it that people were around so we couldn't swim back to the beach and kiss each other for as long as we wanted. It was all I could think about."

He pulled her next to him. "After we met, you were all I ever thought about. My father kept asking me what was wrong and accused me of wandering around in a daze at work. I was literally useless during those three weeks, waiting to get off work to be with you. I didn't know love could be like that."

"Neither did I," she cried. "It frightened me because I knew you were going to leave. There were nights after you left me at the Gatakis' when I wanted to die. That's how I felt last Sunday night when you told me you'd be gone for several days. It brought back the past and I didn't sleep. Can't you tell me about it now? How come Giannina knew about your accident before I did?"

"I'll tell you everything after we drive back up to the villa. We're going to look like lobsters if we don't get out of this sun. You could be pregnant already and don't need any complications because I was too selfish keeping you out here."

She got to her feet. "You haven't kept me out here. I've dreamed of being out here with you and am your willing slave."

Together they gathered their things and walked over to the car parked beneath some trees. On the drive up the road through the trees, Nico told her everything.

"So your uncle has disappeared?"

"I couldn't find him. He's now a wanted man in both countries."

"I can't believe he's caused so much pain to your family over the years. But after what Monika did to us, nothing should surprise me."

"My thoughts exactly."

"I hope your sister can now run the newspaper without any problems. She's such a lovely person."

"She feels the same about you. Now let's go inside for a drink. Then I'd like to spend some time in bed while we plan our honeymoon. We'll leave on ours as soon as Kristos and Dimitra take off."

"We'll only have a week."

"I've given it a lot of thought. Why don't we fly in the private jet to Ottawa to see your publisher. We'll spend a day there while you show me the sights. That will leave us a few more days. What would you like to do with them?" He pulled some drinks out of the fridge and they quenched their thirst.

"If you're asking me seriously, I'd love to go back to Olympia. We only had a day. This time we could stay at that hotel on the hill overlooking the ancient city. You'll never know how much I wanted to be married then and have weeks to spend time in your arms and explore the sites. It's our Greek history, Nico, and it sank deeply into my bones. I'll never get enough of it."

"What a relief, my darling. I was afraid you were going to say London or Paris."

"I'd like to travel to those places, but for our honeymoon I'd rather revisit the spot where I first laid eyes on the Hermes sculpture. It represents my feelings for the man I'd hoped to marry. *You.*" She looked into his eyes. "If you'd seen the look on everyone's face in the hospital lounge when I told them I was your wife... No one could doubt how I feel about you."

He pulled her in his arms. "I happen to know the news that we're married made everyone ecstatic. But no one more than me. For you to announce our marriage proved you've forgiven yourself and unlocked my prison door. It means I have my mermaid back."

"Forever."

They walked through the house to the bedroom. "I've never been this happy in my life. I'm married to the woman I've wanted from the moment I met her, and my beautiful daughter is getting married to a man I love like my own son. It's beyond wonderful."

She threw herself in his arms. "You talk about a prison. That's what I was in all these years, wanting to tell you the truth. I'm not that person any longer."

"We've entered a new phase of life. One exciting aspect is that I get to take a shower with my wife." He grabbed her before she knew what was happening.

"Nico—" she squealed.

"This is just the beginning."

EPILOGUE

DIMITRA'S AUGUST WEDDING DAY had arrived. Alexa drove her to the church early to help her dress in one of the anterooms off the foyer. The ceremony had been scheduled for ten in the morning and Phyllis wheeled their *papoú* to the front of the nave. He wore a new dark blue dress suit with a gardenia and looked splendid.

The well-known Papadakis and Angelis families who'd been in the news recently guaranteed a large crowd. Many of the guests had already arrived. Irena had told Alexa that this was going to be the biggest society wedding Salonica had witnessed in years complete with photographers and various news agencies covering the event.

Alexa had bought a pale peach chiffon knee-length dress with short sleeves and a scooped neckline. She wore a gardenia corsage on her shoulder. Nico liked her hair down so much, she didn't change it. Neither she or Dimitra needed blusher. Excitement had made them both feverish.

Dimitra looked exquisite in a white, A-line lace tulle wedding dress. It was sleeveless with an illusion neckline. The court train gave it a royal elegance. She wore a garland of flowers in her wavy brunette hair. No veil. She didn't want one.

Kristos had sent her a gift of pearls that were his grandmother's. Alexa fastened them around her neck and handed her the wedding bouquet of white roses and gardenias.

"It's almost time, honey. I'm going to find your *papoú*. Your father will be here in a minute to walk you down the aisle. God bless you, darling girl. You look a vision. Kristos is going to think so too."

"I can't believe I'm getting married."

"Are you sure it's what you want?"

"Mama—"

"Don't you know I'm teasing you?" Alexa's

gift to her consisted of a pair of light green peridot earrings that matched her eyes. "You look like a princess."

"I feel like one."

She kissed her cheek. "I'll see you in a few minutes." Alexa left the room and hurried down the aisle to the front of the church. Her grandfather and Phyllis smiled when they saw her coming. Nico's family sat on the other side. Irena had joined them.

Alexa sat on the other side of her grandfather and reached for his hand. "You won't believe how beautiful Dimitra looks in her wedding dress."

"You look like a bride yourself," he whispered.

She gave him a kiss and looked around. The church was filling fast. "Are you really going to be all right while we're both off on our honeymoons?"

"Sweetheart, a week is nothing. I'll be able to keep working on my book, and I have Phyllis. I'm so happy for you and your baby girl, it's put a permanent smile on my face."

"I could never have made it through this life without you and Grandma Iris. I'm so sorry she isn't here."

"But she is."

She nodded. "I'm sure you're right."

Suddenly the organ music started and the priest walked in from a side door resplendent in his robes. Kristos and Yanni followed him, dressed in black tuxedos with gardenias in their lapels. Irena had to be in tears.

Everyone got to their feet as the "Wedding March" played. Alexa turned her head. A quiet gasp escaped her lips at the sight that met her eyes. She'd never forget her beaming daughter who came walking down the aisle with her father. Nico had to be the most magnificent, handsome man in existence.

He wore a black tuxedo, Kristos's choice, with a gardenia in his lapel. All eyes were on the two of them. They looked perfect together. There were no words to describe the feelings bursting inside her. When the two of them reached the front, Nico left his daughter in Kristos's care and walked toward Alexa.

Their eyes fused for a heart-stopping moment. He clasped her hand and never let it go during the nearly hour-long ceremony. The Dance of Isaiah where the husband and wife circled the table three times was particularly moving to Alexa. It was full of symbolism and tradition. By the time the priest gave the final blessing, she was fighting tears.

The married couple turned to the congregation. Dimitra looked at Alexa and Nico across the expanse. Her eyes glowed with happiness and joy. It was all there. Then Kristos looked over at them with the same expression. There were few moments in life more thrilling than this one.

Nico was so moved, he put his arm around Alexa and pulled her closer to him. She looked up at him. "I married you all over again during their ceremony."

He gave her that devastating smile. "I did the same thing. But if you want to know the truth, I felt we were married that night on my cruiser.

"I'm also thinking about the baby we're

going to have, no matter how long it takes for us to get pregnant."

"You don't have to wonder any longer."

"Alexa—" His dark eyes blazed.

She flashed him an illuminating smile. "I did a home test today. We're going to have another baby. We can forget the four months."

"I hoped you didn't mean it, but I didn't want to argue with you at the time. I wanted to marry you so badly, I'm afraid I would have promised you anything. We're really pregnant?"

"Yes, darling, but we'll have to continue this conversation later. Everyone is leaving and we've a reception to attend. Dimitra and Kristos will wonder where we are. She let me know you and I seem to function in a world all our own all the time."

Forgetting everyone else, he bent his head and kissed her. "She got that right. Once our worlds collided, that was it."

"I'm so thankful you asked me to marry you while we were on the yacht. Now another baby is on the way. As it turns out,

Hera didn't win. In the end Io, with all her journeys, was changed back to human form by Zeus and would bear his child, whose descendant would be a great hero.

"That's our story, darling."

* * * * *

LET'S TALK
Romance

For exclusive extracts, competitions
and special offers, find us online:

- facebook.com/millsandboon
- @millsandboonuk
- @millsandboon

Or get in touch on 0844 844 1351*

For all the latest titles coming soon,
visit millsandboon.co.uk/nextmonth

*Calls cost 7p per minute plus your phone company's price per
minute access charge